"You're obser...

"I like watching y... hair off Shelby's ...urprising, quick and intimate gesture that made her mouth go dry. "You stand out in a crowd."

"You, too," she managed to whisper.

His penetrating stare unnerved her nearly as much as his proximity.

He was related to her enemy.

He shouldn't fascinate her. She wasn't one of those women who went after bad boys, hoping to change them. She wasn't intrigued by danger or darkness.

And more turmoil she certainly didn't need.

But she didn't step back. If anything, this endeavor of justice was about standing her ground, standing up for her parents, who couldn't endure alone.

She wasn't about to retreat now....

Dear Reader,

Much as the South is my home, my culture—really, my world—I *love* New York City. At the first step on the pavement, I was astounded by the lights, crowds, sounds and smells. After a few visits, I began to appreciate the mix of cultures, the organized bustle, the glory of the back-alley restaurant, and the utter, complete realization that *this* is where everything happened.

So what better place to explore the illusive concept of justice?

The romantic notion of Robin Hood has been a mythical dream of a variety of cultures for several hundred years. The idea of the oppressed and powerless being triumphant over the establishment— no matter how corrupt—is an an idea with Blaze-worthy sexiness.

So, here we are.

Shelby and Trevor will introduce you to my little Manhattan gang trying to mix romance and justice. Shelby wants to bring the man who swindled her parents out of their retirement savings to justice, and her best buds are eager to help her. Unfortunately, her enemy is her new lover's brother. Is getting revenge worth risking the love of her life?

I hope you'll join me for the entire Flirting with Justice trilogy. Be sure to look for Victoria's story, *Breathless on the Beach,* coming in July.

Happy reading!

Wendy Etherington

Wendy Etherington

SIZZLE IN THE CITY

TORONTO NEW YORK LONDON
AMSTERDAM PARIS SYDNEY HAMBURG
STOCKHOLM ATHENS TOKYO MILAN MADRID
PRAGUE WARSAW BUDAPEST AUCKLAND

Recycling programs
for this product may
not exist in your area.

ISBN-13: 978-0-373-79689-2

SIZZLE IN THE CITY

This edition published by arrangement with Harlequin Books S.A.

For questions and comments about the quality of this book please contact us at Customer_eCare@Harlequin.ca.

® and TM are trademarks of the publisher. Trademarks indicated with ® are registered in the United States Patent and Trademark Office, the Canadian Trade Marks Office and in other countries.

www.Harlequin.com

Printed in U.S.A.

ABOUT THE AUTHOR

Wendy Etherington was born and raised in the deep South—and she has the fried-chicken recipes and NASCAR ticket stubs to prove it. An author of nearly thirty books, she writes full-time from her home in South Carolina, where she lives with her husband, two daughters and an energetic shih tzu named Cody. She can be reached via her website, www.wendyetherington.com. Or follow her on Twitter @wendyeth.

Books by Wendy Etherington

HARLEQUIN BLAZE
263—JUST ONE TASTE...
310—A BREATH AWAY
385—WHAT HAPPENED IN VEGAS...
446—AFTER DARK
524—TEMPT ME AGAIN
562—HER PRIVATE TREASURE
587—IRRESISTIBLE FORTUNE

HARLEQUIN NASCAR
HOT PURSUIT
FULL THROTTLE
NO HOLDING BACK (with Liz Allison)
RISKING HER HEART (with Liz Allison)

To get the inside scoop on Harlequin Blaze and its talented writers, be sure to check out blazeauthors.com.

All backlist available in ebook. Don't miss any of our special offers. Write to us at the following address for information on our newest releases.

Harlequin Reader Service
U.S.: 3010 Walden Ave., P.O. Box 1325, Buffalo, NY 14269
Canadian: P.O. Box 609, Fort Erie, Ont. L2A 5X3

1

"There is no such thing as justice—in or out of court."
—*Clarence Darrow, 1936*

Financial Finagling?
by Peeps Galloway, Gossipmonger
(And proud of it!)

Hello, fellow Manhattanites! As tax day approaches, all the corporate yuk-yuks are frantically lining up numbers in neat little columns. *Yawn.* You and I know what *really* matters in this town—power and popularity. And it seems tycoon wannabe Maxwell Banfield finally has it clutched tightly in his overly tanned hands.

He's now the proud owner of The Crown Jewel, a popular luxury hotel on West 42nd Street in Midtown. Presumably, he'll offer the usual glamorous offerings in the hotel's restaurant, Golden.

But the real jewel in the Crown isn't the four-star eatery, it's the thirtieth-floor lounge, where it's rumored '50s movie star Teresa Lawrence once tossed her drink (a very stiff martini) into legendary singer Paul Castono's face, bringing an end to their tumultuous two-year marriage. In a fit of nostalgia (or perhaps the convenience of the notorious private elevator), the high-flyers of stage and screen still occasionally flock to the joint.

Let's hope Mr. Big Talker Banfield can keep his lucrative clientele happy *this time*.

After all, there were some rumors a few years back about a bit of book-diddling that the IRS wouldn't necessarily approve of. Even if that story was proved unsubstantiated, there's nothing wrong with repeating it *here,* is there, kids! Besides, Max has a social cushion and cache many of us would sell our designer bags and shoes for in a heartbeat.

He's heir apparent to his powerful father, the Earl of Westmore (that's the title of nobility held by the Banfield family of England and Wales). According to my compats in London, however, the future earl hasn't exactly lived up to his respected family name, given all his appearances in the tabloids. (And, *oh, dear,* there's yet another one!) It's rumored dear ole Daddy has cut his son off financially. But here he is, doling out cash for a luxury hotel.

Makes one go *hmm*...huh?

Certainly members of the peerage slithering away from a sticky situation has never happened before in *our* just and pristine land. So I'm sure those rumors about Max were, well...fraudulent. *Wink, wink.*

I, your humble squire, just write and wonder. Maybe Max has suddenly got savvy? Maybe he miraculously found thirty million dollars under his sofa cushions? You be the judge, Urbanites. I know I'll be hitting the streets to find out more.

Keep your ears tuned and your gums flapping!

—*Peeps*

"WE HAVE TO DO SOMETHING."

As Shelby Dixon shoved aside the newspaper, she sighed in disgust. "Where'd that crook Banfield get the money to buy a hotel?"

Her best friend Calla Tucker patted her hand in sympathy. "Apparently there are a lot more swindling victims besides your parents."

Victoria Holmes—her other best friend—narrowed her ice-blue eyes. "For thirty mil, there's a hell of a lot more."

Shelby sipped from her coffee mug and knew the bitter taste wasn't the drink she'd been served at Javalicious, where she and her friends gathered most Sunday afternoons in midtown Manhattan.

Though she was originally from Savannah, Shelby had moved to the city to attend culinary school five years ago, started her own catering business after graduation and had no intention of ever leaving. She loved the vibrancy, the chaos and the struggle of the people and its urban maelstrom of clashing cultures and agendas. She'd adjusted to the size of her meager apartment that contrasted sharply with the extreme wealth of some of the homes she'd visited on the job. She'd learned to groan at the tourists gawking, wandering and clogging the subways, streets and cabs. She'd gotten used to the symphony of horns honking and angry shouts in a variety of languages.

She was home.

Moss dripping from lazy swaying palms was more her parents' style.

Thanks to Max Banfield and his fraudulent investment scheme, however, their seaside retirement had become a nightmare instead of a dream. Their savings account was shot, their spirits broken, their new condo on the verge of foreclosure and they were looking to their only daughter for salvation.

"He's got a rich father." Shelby's gaze flicked to the gossip article. "Maybe I could appeal to him."

Victoria shook her head. "You're chasing a dream. Guys like Max never pay. He's practically British royalty. He probably has an army of peons running behind him to clean up his messes."

"Don't be so negative," Calla said, exchanging a sharp look with Victoria. "Just because that lawyer you went out with tried to use you for your marketing contacts and clearly wanted to get his hands on your trust fund, that's no reason to be pissy."

"Sure it is," Victoria asserted.

Calla's eyes turned dreamy as she propped her chin in her palm. "I had a drink in that top-floor lounge last weekend. Very chic. Great lighting, cozy booths and a curving mahogany bar that probably seats fifty."

"Did Frank Sinatra—the ultracool 1950s version—jump out from behind the potted palm and sing you a tune?" Victoria asked.

Calla blinked. "Well, no."

Victoria swirled her finger in the air. "Then, whooppee."

Calla sighed—though not as deeply or hopelessly as Shelby had. "Come to think of it, the bartender was hotter than my date."

"Could we get back to my crisis here?" Shelby interjected. Normally her friends' opposing attitudes—positive for the ethereal blonde Calla and darkly realistic for the ebony-haired Victoria—were helpful. Today, they tried her patience. "We all have enough lousy date stories to fill the Hudson. Table the romance chat. I can't get the cops to do anything about my parents' case. And if I don't find a way to get their money back, they're going to wind up moving in with me."

"Talk about no romance," Victoria said sagely.

Calla bit into her scone—one Shelby had made and sold

to Javalicious on a weekly basis. She'd spent so much time cultivating relationships with local businesses that they cross-promoted and shared temporary employees and suppliers.

Was all that hard work in jeopardy?

Her parents couldn't live with her in her one-bedroom apartment, and she couldn't afford a bigger place, or continue sending them enough money to pay their condo mortgage. She'd already begged the bank for more time, putting up her catering company as collateral. What if she had to liquidate her business and move back home to support her parents?

That was her duty, she supposed, but it would break her heart. There had to be another way.

"How can there be despair and strife when there are delights like this to enjoy?" Calla said, licking blueberry scone crumbs off her lip. "This is your best creation yet, Shel."

Unfortunately, Shelby couldn't appreciate the compliment. "I don't sleep. I bake."

"Strife?" Victoria narrowed her eyes. "What is this? *The Canterbury Tales?*"

"If only," Calla returned. "Then we could call a knight to raise his sword and strike down the tyranny of injustice, rescue the princess from the castle and bring peace and hope to all the land."

"Darling," Victoria began, clearly making strides for patience, "you're a talented travel writer, but surely you're not thinking about moving into fiction."

"I could, you know." Calla nodded for emphasis. "How hard could it be?"

"I'd imagine quite—"

Shelby poked Victoria. "Hang on. Who's the princess in this story?" she asked Calla.

Calla cocked her head. "Your mother, of course."

"Why not me?" At the moment, Shelby figured she could use a knight or two to save the day.

"Because you're the knight," Calla said as if this were obvious.

Shelby and Victoria exchanged frustrated looks.

"Knives I can handle," Shelby said finally. "Swords aren't really my forte."

"And that chain mail would ruin the body-buffing treatment I got last week," Victoria added.

"Yeah." Calla bit her lip. "Maybe you're right. There has to be a better…" Calla's eyes sparked with inspiration. "We'll go Robin Hood."

Victoria peered into Calla's mug. "Did you add whiskey?"

Calla wrapped her hands protectively around the ceramic. "I added coffee, creme and caramel. I'm perfectly sober."

"Yet you suggested we involve Robin Hood in solving Shelby's parents' financial crisis," Victoria reminded her.

Calla scowled. "*You* brought up *The Canterbury Tales.*"

Victoria nodded. "Because *you* started down Fairy Tale Lane."

"I was helping," Calla said, an atypical fierceness infusing her voice. "You, however—"

Shelby, holding up her hand, was beginning to feel like a referee. "Back to Robin Hood. Are we talking the costumes or the concept?"

"The concept, of course," Calla said. "I'm going nowhere in green tights and a short skirt after eating two of these scones."

"But you're suggesting we steal my parents' savings from Max Banfield," Shelby said slowly.

"Robin Hood didn't steal," Calla asserted. "He brought peace and justice to the land."

"By modern standards he was a vigilante," Victoria argued.

"Well, yes." Calla wiped her hands on a napkin. "But he was right, wasn't he? Fighting against the corrupt establishment? Helping people who'd been wronged and had no means or power of retribution? And I'm not suggesting we steal anything. I simply think we should take the law into our own hands. This investment scheme of Max's had to have affected a lot of people. We should find them and talk to them. We should band together."

"Shelby the Caterer and her Unhappy Retirees," Victoria said sardonically.

"We get proof of his swindling," Calla insisted.

"We get proof," Shelby repeated, both skeptical and curious of this obviously crazy idea.

"Sure." Clearly glad to have an eager audience, she leaned forward. "I'm great at research. How different could this be? We talk to his customers and his former clients. This new hotel gives us the perfect excuse. We could observe him, even interview him. I could pretend I'm doing a story on local entrepreneurs. We gather information and get proof that he's a lying, swindling creep."

Victoria's expression remained passionless. "Something nobody in the entire NYPD has been able to do."

"Only because they haven't really tried," Calla said, tossing a glare in her direction.

Shelby had to admit the idea of seeing that creep Max Banfield led off in handcuffs was appealing. But they all had jobs and businesses to run. Not to mention they had absolutely no authority to go poking around a criminal situation. What if Banfield had diplomatic immunity or something in America? Then the cops couldn't touch him, and she and her friends would get thrown in the dungeon for pestering him. "I appreciate you trying to help, Calla. But I have to agree with Victoria. I don't see how a caterer, a travel writer and a PR executive can solve a case the cops can't."

Calla stubbornly lifted her chin. "We can. We just have to—"

Victoria held up her hand. "Ladies, there's an obvious solution to this problem. I'll loan Shelby's parents the money to get by."

Shelby shook her head. "No. No way." When Victoria looked on the verge of insisting, she added, "They can't pay back a loan. The money they got from selling their dry cleaning business went to the down payment on the condo."

"A beachside condo won't be easy to sell these days," Calla said in an I-told-you-so kind of voice.

Shelby scowled. "No kidding."

"Our social lives are in a serious rut," Calla continued. "We need an adventure to break the monotony." She paused and grinned. "Plus, when is revenge against a creepy guy not fun?"

At this, even Victoria seemed intrigued.

Apparently, Shelby was staring desperation right in the eye, since the Robin Hood plan suddenly sounded like a viable option.

Victoria drummed her manicured fingernails on the table. "We've got one other problem."

"What's that?" Shelby asked, tensing.

"Robin Hood was a myth," Victoria said.

Calla cleared her throat. "Well, yes. That's a small wrinkle."

Shelby resisted the urge to drown herself in her latte.

2

"Mr. Banfield, your brother is on line one."

Trevor glanced up from the financial report he'd been reading to see his assistant filling his office doorway.

Hands planted on her ample hips, Florence Windemere scowled. "He's very insistent."

"I'll bet."

Max was, no doubt, caught in yet another mess of his own making. Who else could he call?

"Did he flirt with you again?" he asked Florence.

"Cheeky, that's what he is. Unprofessional, too."

Trevor smiled slightly at the flushed indignation of the woman who'd been his childhood governess after Max had gone off to boarding school at age eight—the year of their parents' divorce. "So was I at one time."

She drew herself to her full five-foot, one-inch height. "You were simply energetic, maybe a bit precocious and certainly a child. He's a grown man."

"He appears to be anyway."

Florence gave him a sage smile. "There comes a time, my boy, when you have to push the baby bird from the nest."

"Would you have given up on me?"

"He's not you."

"Which I, for one, am thankful. He *is* my brother, however."

"Older brother," Florence reminded him significantly as she retreated from the room.

Trevor understood her implication—the older sibling should be wiser, looking out for the younger. Somehow, almost right from the beginning, his family had been turned backward. And they'd all been paying for that quirk of fate ever since.

Bracing himself, Trevor lifted the phone receiver.

"Know anything about the hotel business?" Max asked him casually.

Way too casually.

Recalling the time Max had asked him about the hot-air-balloon business, only to have his ever-ambitious brother ignore his advice and buy four used ones with the ridiculous dream of them bobbing over and around the skyscrapers of Manhattan and/or Paris, Trevor knew he had to nip this blossoming idea in the bud. "It's volatile, labor intensive, multi-faceted and in no way, shape or form an industry you should be involved in."

"Ah." Long pause. "Uh…okay. What'd ya think of that Jets game on Sunday?"

Trevor got a bad feeling in the pit of his stomach.

And not just because the Jets played football and it was the middle of April.

"What've you done?" he asked Max.

"Me?" he asked with affronted innocence that was well practiced and generally effective. "Not a thing. Though I did have a spicy dinner with a hottie from Venezuela last night. Maybe she's got a sister, you could come with us next time."

Max the Pimping Earl. Lovely. "I can get my own dates, thank you. Did you take Ms. Venezuela to a hotel?"

"No. My apartment."

"Did you eat in a hotel restaurant last night?"

"Uh, well— Hmm… Let me think."

He shared genes with this man. It was terrifying.

And since Trevor didn't have time to wait for the how-can-I-save-my-ass Max thought process to play out, he prompted, "Where did you have dinner?"

"I can't quite remember the name," Max said faintly. "It might have been a color."

"What color?"

"Hmm…red, maybe yellow."

"Where were you?"

"The Theatre District?"

"You're not sure?"

"I was half-pissed. We had drinks before at the top-floor lounge."

The Theatre District was clogged full of hotels. But a hotel with a restaurant whose name was a color—red, maybe yellow—and had a bar on its roof?

"Golden."

Max coughed.

It was mostly a tourist place, but the hotel had endured for more than fifty years and the lounge had its moments being hip and interesting, depending on the nostalgic whims of the NYC elite.

"Oh, damn. That's my other line. Gotta go." Max hung up abruptly but not unexpectedly.

Having flown into New York that afternoon from San Francisco, Trevor had grabbed newspapers at the airport, but other than glancing at the headlines in the cab, and answering a few pending emails on his phone, he hadn't delved further.

Max, at least in this country, was not front-page news.

An internet search on Max yielded thousands of hits on an article titled "Financial Finagling" in the *New York Tattletale*. The author's name was Peeps Galloway.

Talk about cheeky.

"Financial guru?" he muttered aloud as he read. "Since when?"

He had to shut his eyes when he reached the part about The Crown Jewel. *Bloody hell,* Max owned a hotel.

Clearly, their mother's most recent husband was gullible as well as rich, as their father had indeed cut off his oldest son financially.

At least publicly.

Trevor forced himself to read the rest, wincing when he read his father's title. He'd probably be getting a call from his secretary by tomorrow. Maybe even the old man himself. The heir apparent had indeed slithered away from several sticky situations, and yet again, it would no doubt be Trevor's responsibility to shove the mess under the rug.

He'd officially become his family's janitor.

Being the second son of the Earl of Westmore—who was related, by some convoluted and ancient way, to George III of England—Trevor had always known he'd have to make his way in the world. Nothing was going to be handed to him.

His brother would one day be the earl, and Trevor was largely superfluous. Like an insurance policy.

Frankly, Trevor had been relieved by his sibling's departure for boarding school and had blossomed under Florence's watchful, caring eye, even as Max fell in with a group of arrogant, troublesome boys who thought their future titles made them invulnerable.

The divorce hit him harder than you was a good excuse he got for his brother's behavior. *He worshipped your mother and doesn't know how to cope without her.* Or, *Max has the pressure of the title on his shoulders.*

During those days Trevor had resented being metaphorically shoved in a drawer and forgotten about, so he'd dreamed of becoming a teacher, then a poet, then a rock star. Thanks to Florence, he eventually learned to play to his advantages—athletic skill, a fair amount of charm, a strong dose of good sense and a trust fund to get virtually any venture started.

So, as his father mourned the loss of his marriage and Max had taken advantage of his distraction, Trevor had decided he'd run his own business. He'd be in control. He'd escape family obligations.

Not so fast, my boy.

Even after he'd left for America in his early twenties, he'd been dragged into Max's troubles. He made excuses. He'd reasoned with his brother. Apparently, no one else could. When his business became financially successful, he'd bailed out Max of several money crises.

Trevor had always understood his actions reflected on the rest of his family, on the ancestry to which he was forever linked by blood. Max loved parties, women and being important.

There were whispers that Trevor was the better successor to the title. That Max would never grow up. Yet, unless the line of succession was somehow eradicated, they were stuck.

Max was more like their mother—flighty and unpredictable. But while she was kind and generous, Max was inherently selfish. He expected others to pick him up when he fell down. Even at an early age, he managed to blame the crayons on the wall or the snags in the tapestries on his "energetic" little brother.

Yet Trevor and Max were bonded by a single truth—neither of them wanted to become their father. The stoic earl. Distant, but devastated by his divorce.

So Trevor had learned discretion and discipline at the stable hand of Florence. Nobody had to explain his partying the night away with hot women, too many cocktails and getting his picture printed in some trashy rag as a result.

Thirty odd years after their home life had imploded, Max had never learned that lesson.

Maybe they all should have realized that the crayons on the wall would lead to lousy financial and business management, gambling debts and embarrassing questions by peers and friends.

Trevor used to be proud that his father looked to him to help his brother, to coach him out of whatever ridiculous mess he'd landed in. There was no real harm in him—other than to his own family. But wasn't there a time to push the baby bird from the nest?

The intercom buzzed, and Florence's voice floated out. "Your father's on the phone."

"Brilliant," Trevor said sarcastically.

Project Robin Hood, Day Four
The Crown Jewel Hotel

A HOTEL SUITE'S BEDROOM wasn't the strangest place Shelby had used as a temporary kitchen and prep area, but it was damn close.

With a metaphorical shrug for the oddities of her job and praying the health inspector didn't make a surprise visit, she removed another tray of mini crab cakes from her warming ovens as the door swung open.

"I'm in with Banfield," Calla said, poking her head around the door.

Shelby set the hot tray on a trivet. "That was fast. You've barely been here fifteen minutes."

Calla grinned. "I'm pretty impressed myself." She pursed her lips. "'Course it helps that he's a dense and raving egomaniac."

"It sure can't hurt. Is Victoria here yet?"

"Just walked in."

"Make sure she stows her sharklike tendencies. She might scare him off."

"He seems pretty much dazzled by boobs, a heartbeat and a smile. V could manage him in her sleep."

Transferring crab cakes to a serving platter, Shelby felt a rush of excitement. This crazy Robin Hood plan might actually work.

Asking questions of the well-connected crowd, Shelby and her friends had learned Max was throwing a cocktail party in his suite to celebrate the "Under New Management" kickoff of the hotel. Victoria managed to get invited under the guise of offering PR services and promising to bring the press—aka Calla. She'd also suggested Shelby as the caterer, which Max had jumped on, presumably because his kitchen was currently understaffed, though Shelby suspected her undercut rates had pushed her to the top of the list.

She and her friends were going to mingle and listen, hopefully instigating themselves in Max's life and business, which would, presumably, lead to proof of his financial schemes. Or at least give them a new angle to take to the police.

Know thy enemy as thyself, right?

Calla was going to offer to interview him for a piece in *City Magazine,* one of her regular clients. The fact that she'd already secured their quarry's cooperation made Shelby all the more grateful for her friends' support.

"You're the best," she said to Calla as she added sprigs of lettuce and lemon wedges to decorate the platter.

"Remember this was all my idea," her friend said saucily as she flipped her wheat-colored ponytail over her shoulder and turned to leave.

Moving to follow, Shelby caught a glimpse of herself in the mirror on the wall. She'd made an effort to tame her wavy, shoulder-length auburn hair into artful curls. Only to have the thick mess turn frizzy beneath the heat of the ovens and the sweaty job of hauling all her equipment from her delivery van to the penthouse suite.

Oh, well. She had Calla and Victoria to dazzle Banfield. As long as she kept him and his guests fed, she'd done her job for the night.

Balancing the serving tray in one hand, she managed to open the door and ease her way into the main room without dropping anything.

At least until she hit what felt like a solid wall. With a grunt of frustration, she watched two precious crab cakes tumble toward the floor.

She was going to go broke saving her parents from financial ruin.

"Pardon me," said a silky, English-accented voice.

"No, problem," Shelby said, quickly glancing up, "I'll—"

She nearly dropped the entire tray as she got a look at the man attached to the exquisite voice.

Wavy black hair, blue eyes like the depths of the deepest sea and a trim physique encased in a meticulously tailored charcoal-colored suit.

Damn. Why doesn't my hair look better? was the only thought she could manage.

"I'll keep this one if you don't mind," he said.

Which one? *Me?* She was nodding before she'd even completed the thought.

As he straightened, she noticed the crab cake he was raising toward his mouth.

Wow, he has a great mouth, too.

Raising her gaze to his eyes, a jolt of sheer pleasure shot through her. She got the sense that he understood the effect he had on her. Or else he really liked crab cakes.

After chewing and swallowing, he sipped his cocktail—a martini with two olives—then smiled.

Though his eyes were steady as a rock, there was something fun and alluring about his smile. As if the rest of his perfection was hard-won. As if rebellion was natural and refinement a birthright he'd reluctantly accepted.

"You're the chef?" he asked.

"Yes," she managed to answer without stuttering.

"More crab than fluff," he commented. "Rare at these gatherings."

"I grew up in Savannah. It's a Southern-pride thing."

"Well deserved." He angled his head. "And the accent fits. I got the sense you weren't from here."

"You, either."

He nodded. "I was raised in London."

"That fits." Given the nature of her undercover plan, she wondered at the quirk of fate that had presented her with a flesh and blood James Bond in the middle of her investigative adventure. "Shelby Dixon," she said, holding out her hand.

"Trevor," the man said as he enveloped her small hand in his elegant, long-fingered one.

Their gazes held as they shook.

Shelby would have been happy to let their closeness linger for the next decade or two, but she was supposed to be working, both as a caterer and a spy.

A quick scan of the room noted several new guests. Max had assured her there would be no more than fifteen, but they were pushing twenty-five. Good thing she'd made extra hors d'oeuvres.

Drooling over the luscious Trevor No-Last-Name-Given would have to wait.

And why hadn't he given a last name anyway? Wasn't that odd? He was probably Max's bookie or possibly something even more nefarious. But by the time she'd considered this and turned to question him, he was walking away…directly toward Max.

The hotel owner-swindler welcomed Trevor with a hug and a broad grin.

"Well, damn," Shelby grumbled.

She should have expected this turn, as no man could be that perfect and have moral standards, too. If he was Max's investment recruiter, it was easy to see how the lousy crook had gotten his hands on thirty-million bucks. There was probably a line outside his office door to get in on the next deal.

Guests were starting to come to her to get a crab cake, so she reluctantly tore her gaze from Max and Trevor and roamed the room with her tray. After a while, she retreated to the bedroom to load up again, adding prosciutto-wrapped grilled-chicken bites, as well.

She passed Calla chatting up the hotel manager and hoped her friend was getting insightful info to use in their quest to bring Max and his schemes down. Full bellies and a cocktail or two were secret weapons in getting people to talk incessantly. Maybe she should share that tidbit with law enforcement.

She found Victoria next to the windows of the twenty-ninth-floor suite and offered her appetizer selections to her fellow conspirator, whose eyes were uncharacteristically dazed.

"I love New York," Victoria said, staring in Trevor's direction.

"He has an English accent, too."

Victoria's eyelashes fluttered as her face glowed with pleasure. "Oh, my."

"However…" Shelby said sharply, striving to bring Victoria back to her senses, "he seems pretty friendly with Max, so no matter how beautiful he is, he's now moved to second on the list of suspicious characters in this room."

"He's number one in my book," Victoria said, licking her lips.

"Helloo?" Shelby waved her hand in front of her friend's face. "Revenge? Vigilante justice? Any of these concepts sound familiar? *Max* is Project Robin Hood's Enemy Number One. He's our Sheriff Nottingham, our Al Capone. And anybody who cozies up to him is an accessory simply on principle."

"You're right," Victoria said slowly. She took a step in Trevor's direction. "I'll do some up-close and personal investigation."

Shelby caught her friend's arm. "Not so fast, Eliot Ness. I think observation is the best plan for now. Besides, I've already made contact."

"So?"

"I saw him first."

Victoria crossed her arms over her chest. "Really?"

"His name is Trevor."

"Trevor what?"

Blushing, Shelby shrugged.

"You can't be that committed to him. A conversation that didn't last long enough to get his full name? Get a hold of yourself. I thought he was Enemy Number Two."

Even more embarrassed, Shelby recalled her conversation that morning with her mom, who'd sounded so tired and defeated. The doctors had increased her anti-anxiety meds, and she was having a hard time adjusting. Not daring to glance at the object of her and Victoria's conversation, she rolled her shoulders. "He is," she said firmly.

And he was.

Except he was also the most beautiful man she'd ever laid eyes on.

No one could tell her fate wasn't enjoying a hilarious and cruel joke at her expense.

"Go chat him up," Shelby said to Victoria. "Maybe you can get his last name."

"Oh, no. This one's all yours." With a knowing smile, Victoria took Shelby's tray and glided away.

Well, she'd asked for it. She ought to be woman enough to take it.

After sending a glare toward Victoria's retreating back, Shelby started across the room toward Max and Trevor. Along the way, several guests stopped her to compliment the culinary offerings and ask if there were more. She assured everyone there was and indicated Victoria, who, despite her smart-ass tendencies, was one of her best and most loyal friends.

A definite BFF, since she'd gracefully conceded the path to Trevor and was currently doing Shelby's job, as well.

Trevor is a bad, bad man, her conscience reminded her.

Actually, she didn't know that for sure. Probable, but not certain.

She could only help her parents through this hardship if she knew the facts. This investigation was her duty as a daughter. This was business, not romance.

On the way toward her prey, she noted an unbalanced collection of the female population surrounding Trevor and Max. This phenomenon could be easily explained. Because, while Max had Trevor's dark coloring, his eyes were a muddy brown, he was shorter and more rotund than the sophisticated Englishman she'd met earlier, and there was a distinct shiftiness in his eyes.

Wow. She really needed to focus on what she was supposed to be doing here.

Yet another guest stopped her. "I'm dying for one of those delicious crab cakes," the clearly desperate woman pleaded.

Shelby cast a glance at her gorgeous goal. Like she'd get his attention in her wilted white chef's apron and limp hair anyway. However, he'd seemed to enjoy the crab cakes… "Okay, sure," she said to the desperate guest.

Retreating to the prep room, she assembled another tray of crab, but halfway through her task, she was startled by hot and mysterious Trevor walking in, then closing the door behind him.

"How do you know Max?" he asked without delay.

"I'm his caterer." His curiosity only furthered her suspicions of him. He was protective of Max. Meeting that alluring, blue-eyed gaze boldly, she added, "How do *you* know Max? You two seem like old friends."

"We know each other well," he returned vaguely as he moved toward her. "What about the writer and the icy brunette? You're friends with them."

"How do you know that?" she accused, wincing, as she realized she'd inadvertently confirmed his assumptions.

Some secret agent she was.

He smiled, confident and tempting. "I saw you talking to them earlier, just as you obviously saw me with Max. The brunette even refilled your food tray."

"You're observant."

"I like watching you." He brushed a strand of hair off her forehead in a surprising, quick and intimate gesture that made her mouth go dry. "You stand out in a crowd."

"You, too," she managed to whisper.

His penetrating stare unnerved her nearly as much as his proximity.

He was a friend of her enemy. He shouldn't fascinate her. She wasn't one of those women who went after bad boys, hoping to change them. She wasn't intrigued by danger or darkness.

And more turmoil she certainly didn't need.

But she didn't step back. If anything, this endeavor of justice was about standing her ground, standing up for her parents, who couldn't endure alone.

She wasn't about to retreat now.

3

TREVOR FOUGHT AGAINST THE impulse to slide his arms around the beautiful redheaded caterer. To find out the source of the worry behind her intriguing hazel eyes. To forget that he was only present to save Max from yet another of his follies.

But he was certainly losing the battle.

He wanted a taste of her as surely as he'd savored her food. Not so many years ago, he'd have indulged in the impulse to sweep her from the party, no matter about either of their obligations.

But he'd grown up, grown smarter and more successful along the way. Yet, as hard-won as his control had been, Shelby Dixon, with her fiery locks and petite frame, somehow tested it.

Reminding himself there were things in life more important than his own pleasure, he stepped back.

"You weren't suspicious when the owner of a hotel asked an outside service to cater his party?" he asked, hoping to get the conversation back to business.

She shrugged. "He's shorthanded in the kitchen." She paused a long moment before adding, "And my friend Victoria—the brunette who helped me earlier—is looking to get his PR business. I offered to help out."

That explanation made sense. He might be reading too much into this party and everyone attending…but then he had plenty of reasons for being suspicious of Max and anyone in his circle. "You'll certainly get future bookings after tonight, including ones from me."

"Good to know. What business are you in?"

This lot was a curious one. "Transportation, but I was thinking of personal needs."

Her eyes widened.

He smiled. "Mmm. Those, too. Though at the moment I was referring to social events. How do you feel about dinner parties?"

"As long as the check clears, I feel pretty great about them."

Beautiful and practical. He was smitten already. "A wise decision."

She walked over to a canvas bag sitting on the desk and pulled out a cell phone. "What day were you thinking about?" she asked, tapping the screen.

"Well, I—"

The blonde who appeared in the doorway was the writer Trevor had met earlier. "Shelby, where's—" She glanced at him before directing her attention to Shelby. "The guests are asking about crab cakes and lettuce wraps. You'd think these people hadn't eaten in a week."

"Free food brings out the animal in everybody," Trevor commented.

"Nice," the blonde said, pulling a tiny spiral notebook and pen from her blazer pocket. "Mind if I use that line?"

Trevor made an old-fashioned bow. "Be my guest."

She blinked. "Hmm. Hot *and* polite." She tucked the note-book away with the same efficiency in which she'd retrieved it. "More crab and wraps soon," she said, pointing to Shelby.

"I'm bringing out the last tray now," she said as the blonde backed from the room.

Shelby cleared her throat. "That's my other friend, Calla—she's a travel and lifestyle magazine writer."

"So I heard. She attempted to interrogate me earlier."

An uncomfortable expression crossed Shelby's lovely face. "Interrogate? That's an odd description."

"But apt."

There was certainly something unusual about this trio of beautiful women appearing in Max's life, but he'd be damned if he could figure out what.

The title? Not likely. His father was hale and hearty and likely to hang around several more decades. And the status of dating the future Earl of Westmore didn't hold quite the same cache in New York as it did in London. Film or sports stars got much more notice.

The ladies also didn't seem after money. Good thing, since Max didn't have any, and would likely have less after a few months in the hotel business.

Plenty of people were eager for any work they could get these days. Maybe these women were simply hungry. In NYC ambition was practically a sport, after all.

Yet he didn't trust them—he didn't trust anyone easily. Never had, even without The Max Episodes to reflect on. People had used him many times over in an effort to get access to his powerful family, so he wasn't anxious to reveal too much to Shelby, no matter his attraction to her.

"You and your friends are quite a team," he said as she tucked her phone away and went back to loading her tray of appetizers.

"We stick together." She straightened with her tray resting expertly on her shoulder. "Much like you do with your friends, I bet."

Trevor nodded. "Naturally," he said, though he was embarrassed to acknowledge, even privately, that he didn't have a huge group of friends. He had acquaintances, business partners and lovers, but not a whole lot in-between.

Well, other than family.

He had an avalanche of family.

"The crab-cake devotees await," she said, heading toward the door, which he opened. She cast a glance at him. "This is the last of them, so I may need a discreet exit in a few minutes. Are you available?"

"Absolutely."

She handed him a business card as she strode from the room. "Call me when you decide about that dinner party."

He glanced at the card and sighed. A strawberry dripping in decadent chocolate sauce dominated the background. Shelby's name and contact information were printed in black ink in the corner.

The idea of keeping his distance was a lost cause.

At nearly midnight, her delivery van pulled into the hotel's loading dock. Shelby and her friends moved her equipment and reflected on a successful, if somewhat frustrating, catering event.

The food—and service, thanks to Calla and Victoria—had been first-rate. The investigation had only led to more questions than answers.

Predictably, she'd run out of crab cakes and had to fill in with more chicken wraps and cheese-stuffed tomato skewers. She'd finished the party with luscious dark-chocolate truffles filled with raspberry creme. Max and his guests had loved every bite. She'd handed out cards by the dozens. Then, at some point, despite his promise to protect her from the crab-crazed crowd, Trevor had disappeared.

Poof, like a magician.

Or the longtime friend of a crook.

He was sneaky, no doubt about it. Somehow, while complimenting, flirting and getting all kinds of details about her, her friends and their motives, he'd avoided revealing his last name, his true relationship with Max or much of anything about his own business. "Transportation? Bah."

For all she knew, he could be up to his gorgeous neck in trafficking—and she didn't mean black-market seafood.

"Sister, we have bigger problems than the Beautiful Brit," Calla pointed out. She handed over an armload of dirty serving platters. "I didn't get a whole lot out of Max."

"Of course you didn't," Victoria said drily, storing the last of the warming trays on the rack installed in the back of the van. "He's a *swindler*. He's an expert at deceit and misdirection."

"But I'm a professional information gatherer." Calla frowned. "He bragged a lot, which I expected, but refused to set up a time for my *City Magazine* interview, even though he'd agreed to do it."

"Empty promises," Victoria said.

"And," Calla continued, "he never gave many details about his plans or his partners of this new venture, if there are any."

"We did overhear the information about the investors' meeting scheduled for next week," Victoria reminded them.

"Investors for what, though?" Calla asked.

"Whatever his backup plan might be after he screws up this hotel thing." Victoria dusted off her immaculate black pantsuit as she climbed out of the van. "It's obvious he doesn't have a clue about the business. I talked to him for three minutes and knew that much. And he had cold eyes, dismissive, arrogant."

"I didn't see that," Shelby said, surprised by her friend's assessment.

Victoria waved off her concern. "Not important. I'm just put off by the subterfuge of this whole thing. I prefer the direct route, as you know."

Calla fisted her hand at her side. "We need to get invited

to that investors meeting." With a sigh, she sat on the tailgate of the van. "Somehow."

Shelby heard her own frustrated reflection echoed by her buddies, but her regrets were more personal. She knew she should be focused on Max, but Trevor dominated her thoughts. She'd all but thrown herself into the man's arms at one point. "Why did I blab to him like a starry-eyed gossip?"

Calla stared at her. "Max?"

"Trevor," Victoria answered before Shelby could. "And you didn't. You gave him your cover story."

Shelby resisted the urge to sink onto the floor of the van. "And my business card, my last name and, oh, yeah, yours and Calla's names and what you were doing at the party."

"What we were *allegedly* doing," Victoria insisted.

Shelby recalled the gleam in Trevor's eyes—and not just the carnal one. "He knew we were up to something."

"So?" Calla countered. "*He's* probably up to something, and Max definitely is. We're going to find out what. Remember, to think like a shark, you have to swim with the fishes."

Victoria planted her hands on her hips. "That metaphor is all wrong."

"Do sharks even think?" was Shelby's instinctive question.

"Don't sharks *eat* fish?" Victoria added.

Calla waved her hand. "Doesn't matter."

"It does if you're the fish," Shelby said.

"Which we are not." Calla helped Shelby out of the van, then they closed the doors. "We are women, hear us *holla*."

"That's roar," Victoria countered.

Calla shook her head. "Trust me, it's *holla*. I recently did a piece on urban slang."

"It doesn't matter if we bellow, shriek or wail," Shelby said, leaning against the van. "We'll still be two steps behind, and I still won't know anything about that Trevor character."

Calla patted her shoulder. "Don't worry about him. I'm all

over that." She cocked her head. "I've seen him somewhere before. I just can't place the circumstance."

"And I'll start asking around about the investors' meeting and what it's for." Victoria slid her arm around Shelby's waist in a rare show of physical affection. "Max will need money for this new project, so my family will be high on the list. Don't stress out. We're going to get this guy."

Shelby leaned against Victoria and at the same time grasped Calla's hand. Her friends' support meant everything. They'd been through bad breakups, job losses and family drama. They'd get through this crisis with the same bond of solidarity they'd shared for years.

Footsteps echoing on the ramp leading from the hotel brought Shelby out of her reverie.

She exchanged brief, wary glances with her friends before peeking her head around the corner of her van to see the source of the interruption.

Trevor.

"Good evening, ladies," he said as he approached the van.

Shelby, along with her coconspirators, were struck dumb by the breathtaking sight of him.

His glossy hair gleamed blue-black beneath the streetlight. His suit—which had to be handmade—fit his trim body and broad shoulders to perfection. His dark blue eyes glowed with power.

"Nice party," he said, and stopped directly in front of Shelby.

"Ah…thanks."

After quick elbow jabs into her sides, Shelby's best buds fled like vegans confronted with rare steak. They mumbled excuses about checking the suite for leftover supplies, then disappeared.

Ironically similar to Transportation Trevor's exit from the party earlier.

"Where did you go?" Shelby asked—okay, maybe she accused. "You said you'd defend me if the crab-cake masses attacked, and you were nowhere to be found when the goods ran out."

"Sorry. I had to take an important call."

"From whom?"

He moved in, his tempting body nearly brushing hers and laid his palm against her cheek. "My father."

"Oh." Given the state of her family, Shelby wasn't oblivious to the idea that others faced the possibility of caring for their parents. "Is he okay?"

"Irate, but that's normal. So, yes."

The look in his eyes, plus his warm hand against her skin scattered her thoughts. "I'm glad, but what—"

Before she could draw another breath, his lips were against hers.

He touched nothing but her lips with his mouth and her cheek with his hand. The moment drew out, romantic, alluring and teasing, as if he was waiting for her approval, as if he knew he'd crossed a line, but was confident he wouldn't be shoved back.

Shelby had no intention of pushing him away.

She didn't know him; she suspected him. Of all manner of things.

But she moved closer. There was something about him she couldn't dismiss or forget. She wrapped her arms around his neck. Leaning into him, she initiated another kiss.

He responded with hunger and experience, angling his head and seducing her mouth with deep strokes of his tongue. Her spine seemed to melt, like chocolate in a double boiler.

She inhaled his warm, sandalwood scent, felt the heat and hardness of his body. He enveloped her like a blanket, though she knew there were layers of unknown to explore, feelings beyond pleasure and comfort.

When they separated, their gazes locked, their breathing labored, she could only manage one comment.

"All in all, it was a pretty damn great party."

4

Party Like a Hotel Magnate
by Peeps Galloway, Gossipmonger
(And proud of it!)

A quick drop-in before your weekend in the Hamptons...

Oh, not spending your days at the luxurious retreat of the well-to-do?

Maybe you're drowning your sorrows over your tax bill at the local pub. Or possibly spending your generous refund at Bloomys or Barney's? (I hear there's a fabulous shoe sale at the later—just ask for Damon.)

Whatever your weekend plans...never fear, dear readers, I'll make either your shopping or your weekend shift at the tourist trap turn-and-burn palatable.

Speaking of tasty, I hear Max Banfield had an *ooh, la, la* soireé at his new hotel, The Crown Jewel, last night. Crab, so fresh from the sea the claws were still twitching, and chicken lettuce wraps were among the food offerings, with the night ending in raspberry creme-filled chocolate truffles.

Need I say yum?

No, I'm sure you have your own version of lusciousness to reflect upon.

Didn't I tell you about Damon?

—Peeps

Hotel magnate?

Was that a promotion over financial guru?

Trevor tossed aside the newspaper Florence had set on his desk.

Instead of worrying about his brother, he stared out his window, where the streets below teemed with the usual afternoon Manhattan chaos. He'd planned to spend the weekend at his house in the Hamptons, but instead of anticipating the escape and relaxation, his thoughts turned to the sensational kiss he and Shelby had enjoyed the night before.

He'd crossed a line with her and didn't regret it in the least.

He should have been concentrating on Max and tempering his latest mistake—or at least diminishing its press-worthy moments—but instead Trevor'd found his attention straying to the stunning caterer all night. The usual responsibility to his family paled in comparison to her vibrancy and glowing smile. As practicality seemed to be her mantra, he sensed even she wouldn't approve of him being so distracted.

He was reminded of the genetic, and sometimes irrational, impulses he'd inherited. Impulses that ruled his mother's life and ones even his stodgy father had indulged in long enough to produce him and Max.

Perhaps Trevor's rebel past wasn't so easily left behind.

And yet he'd been self-possessed enough to recognize the determination in Shelby's eyes. Just as his mother had resolved to possess jewels, clothes and husbands, Shelby had her own goal in mind.

What, he wasn't entirely sure. But it somehow involved Max.

He'd confirmed only two things the night before—Max's financial windfall had indeed come in the form of their latest, wealthy, clearly gullible stepfather. And their father was monumentally annoyed about his name appearing in the American gossip rags.

Surely you can control this situation, Trevor, his father had said on a cell-phone call from his office in London. *I have important issues before Parliament to address in the coming weeks. I don't have time to explain this nonsense.*

I'll handle it, sir.

He's a grown man, his father had continued. *Reason with him. You're the only one he listens to.*

But Max didn't listen to him. He didn't take his advice or take responsibility. He wasn't even a grown man. Not really.

He went to Vegas and blew money. He ran up debts at the London card clubs and pubs.

In some respects, Trevor knew he'd failed his family. At the same time, he had the sense to not remind his father that *he* was the one who'd married and divorced the flighty, but beautiful woman who'd created Max, who was, in turn, creating the present problems.

You could be the first son, his conscience reminded him firmly. *Then you'd be required to follow in the earl's footsteps as well as adhere to every edict that fell from his lips.*

Not that Max was following this ancient rule.

Still, there were significant blessings in Trevor's life. Starting and ending without the burden of an earldom. He had his future well in hand, and it didn't include addressing Parliament, clamoring around a moldy country castle or lording over a London flat, no matter how tony the address.

He had a business to run.

With that bracing reminder reverberating in his mind, he turned back to his desk and the pile of contracts awaiting his signature.

Before he'd read more than a few paragraphs, the intercom on his desk beeped. "Shelby Dixon is here, sir," Florence said. "She doesn't have an appointment but assures me you'll see her."

Not only would he see her, he craved her presence.

He took a second to lift his eyes heavenward and repent any resentful thoughts of the last week. Since they were certainly numerous, Florence buzzed through again before he'd managed to respond.

"I'll see Ms. Dixon," he said into the intercom with what he hoped was a calm, professional tone.

In the intervening moments, his heart kicked against his ribs; his body hummed. He remained standing out of pride. She'd somehow found him, and he wasn't sure if he was impressed or concerned.

Attitude first, Shelby stalked into the room. She performed a mock curtsy in front of his desk. "Your Lordship."

"Ah…no." Suppressing a wince, he paused to drink in the amazing, furious sight of her before extending his hand toward the chair in front of his desk. He waited until she sat before he lowered himself into his own seat. "I don't have a title, though the doorman at my apartment building does persist in calling me Mr. Banfield. I prefer Trevor."

"Your father is the Earl of Westmore," she accused, her eyes more vividly green than the night before.

Perhaps rage brought out the distinctive color?

"He is," Trevor said calmly. "I'm the second son, however, so I'm only significant if my older brother dies." As his blunt words registered, shock flittered across her face. "No worries, he's in excellent health."

"Your older brother is Maxwell Banfield."

Since the connection had been made, he saw no reason to deny it. Though, like many times in the past, he wanted to. "He is."

"And you were at the party last night because…?"

"I was toasting my brother's success."

"You didn't tell me he was your brother."

He smiled. "Didn't I?"

"No."

"It hardly matters."

She crossed her arms over her chest. "I think it does."

Trevor shrugged. He loved her suspicious nature. He liked that she wasn't buying his story completely, and she certainly didn't appear impressed by his lineage. She should be sucking up to him, hoping for an introduction to his influential family or at least pushing for a booking.

Instead, she seemed genuinely, personally annoyed.

Wasn't that great?

"Did Max pay his catering bill?" he asked, wondering who exactly she was mad at and why.

"Yes."

"Did he come on to you?"

"No."

"I'm sorry. He's always had questionable taste in women."

"I didn't want him—" She narrowed her eyes. "You're pretending not to understand why I'm here and pissed off."

He reached deep for an innocent expression. "Why would I do that?"

"I have no idea."

As much as he was attracted to her, and had planned to call her with both a dinner invitation and a quote on catering a business event, he didn't know her well enough to throw open the family-closet door and let her see inside. He didn't want her to suspect how big an embarrassment Max was to the family, or how Trevor was convinced this latest venture would be yet another failure.

Of course if Max's check didn't clear, or Shelby was a big fan of gossip mags, then his efforts at subterfuge would fail no matter what Trevor did or didn't do. "Well, I'm pleased you're here, but I'm truly in the dark about why you're aggravated."

"You kissed me."

He didn't have to pretend to be surprised by that accusation. "I've been complimented heavily in the past on my technique. Can you be specific about why you're disappointed?"

Leaning across his desk, she propped her chin on her fist. "Can you explain why even absurd questions sound intelligent when spoken with an English accent?"

Her sass and directness were enthralling—as well as her proximity.

He tilted toward her. Their faces were bare inches apart. "That's a fascinating debate. Why don't we discuss it over dinner tonight?"

She simply shook her head. "Not so fast, Your Lordship. You kissed me while deliberately keeping your identity a secret. In fact, the only reason I found you was because Calla never throws anything away, and she uncovered a magazine article about you landing a high-dollar contract last year." She raised her eyebrows. "At least I know you transport legitimate goods now."

"What did you think I transported?"

"Could've been anything."

"Like knockoff designers bags, I suppose."

"Yeah, maybe, but I don't like those. It's real or nothing for me. I buy vanilla from Madagascar, for heaven's sake. I was thinking more pharmaceutical for your possibly illegal transportation business."

Terrific. The woman he had a massive crush on thought he

was a drug dealer. "All the more reason for dinner. There's a lovely Italian restaurant down the street."

She angled her head, considering him. The anger had been doused, replaced by interest. "Why didn't you want me to know who you were?"

"I don't like to advertise my family background. It tends to make people act...unusually."

"Suck-ups."

With a satisfied grin, he nodded. "Precisely."

"Why doesn't your brother talk like you?"

"Max puts on an American accent. He likes to blend."

By the way she cocked her head, Trevor assumed she found that as odd as he did, but he didn't really want to discuss Max's idiosyncrasies.

"I like your accent better." Her eyes smoldered into golden. "Is this Italian place down the street Giovanni's?"

Fascinated by the way her eyes changed in rhythm with her mood, he slid his finger down her arm. "It is."

A smile teased her lips. "I could eat."

"Excellent. Perhaps we could also work on my kissing technique. I'd hate to be a disappointment the second time around."

"Were you planning this practice during dinner?"

"I could wait till after. Or be persuaded to before."

Her gaze dropped to his mouth. "Let's see if the pesto sauce is as good as I remember."

Pleasure and anticipation raced down his spine. Their chemistry had been pretty electric the night before—maybe even more so because of the suspicion between them. "I'll speak to the chef personally."

"His name is Mario."

He walked around the desk and assisted her to her feet. "He's not your knife-wielding cousin or boyfriend, is he?"

"My cousin lives in Fort Lauderdale and runs a car wash, and I don't have a boyfriend."

"I always thought the men of New York had good taste. Clearly, I've been misinformed." He opened his office door and allowed Shelby to proceed him. "I'm leaving, Florence."

"For the day?" His secretary's pink painted mouth rounded in shock. "It's barely after five."

"It's Friday. Go home. Enjoy yourself."

"Yes, I remember how. Do *you?*"

Trevor narrowed his eyes briefly as he passed Florence's desk. "Of course I do." The last thing he needed was Florence blabbing about his obsessive tendencies. Success didn't come without sacrifice, after all.

The irony that his secretary wanted him to slow down and have babies she could spoil, while his mother's worst nightmare was becoming a grandmother wasn't lost on him.

"But you'll miss out on your workaholic merit badge for the week," she called after him.

"Good night, Florence," he said, refusing to rise to her critique.

To his relief, Shelby laughed. "And here I thought we had nothing in common. My friends and assistants are always trying to get me to work less and play more."

"Easy to do when it's not your company on the line."

"Exactly."

Trevor pressed the button for the elevator, which arrived immediately.

"Is your brother a crook?" Shelby asked abruptly.

He nearly stumbled. It was rare for him to be knocked off stride, and this woman had done it twice in ten minutes. "No. Why do you ask?"

She shrugged as the elevator doors slid closed. "Just curious."

CALLA WALKED AWAY FROM a lovely spring evening, through the police-station door and into chaos.

The large, pitiful waiting room, painted a dingy gray and containing no more than ten folding chairs, strained at all the emotions and activity.

In one corner, a group of people stood in a circle, holding hands and praying. A trio of women cried in the other. A pair of children bounced and giggled on their chairs as a harried-looking woman stood nearby and yakked into her cell phone.

Lording over the masses, a bored-looking clerk sat behind a high, imposing faded wood counter and flipped through a magazine.

Lady Justice could hardly be proud.

But then Calla figured the police had a mostly thankless, as well as dangerous, job. They'd no doubt be grateful for her help.

Shifting her briefcase strap on her shoulder, she approached the counter. "I need to speak to someone in the fraud department."

The clerk never looked up. "Appointment?"

You needed to make an appointment to report a crime? "No, it's rather urgent. If you could just—"

"Is anybody in immediate danger?"

"Yes, I guess so. My friend Shelby's parents trusted this guy with their life savings, then he took off for parts unknown, but then we—Shelby, me and our other friend Victoria—read an article last week about how he'd bought a hotel right here in Manhattan. So, you can imagine how surprised we were. Where did he get the money to buy something like that?" She jabbed her finger on the counter to emphasize her indignation. "On the backs of gullible seniors, that's where. So, as you can see, it's imperative that I talk to somebody right away."

The clerk looked up, her expression weary. "Is somebody about to die?"

Calla blinked. "Uh…no, but—"

"Everybody's busy." The clerk's attention went back to her magazine.

It was no wonder Max Banfield was running around free as a bird.

But Calla had been a newspaper reporter in her hometown of Austin before she'd moved to New York and become a features writer. She'd navigated the turbulent waters of Texas politics, she'd interviewed presidents and kings, she'd even gone on safari in Africa last year. And she knew charm would get her further than bullying.

"I know you're extremely busy," she said sweetly to the clerk. "But I'm in a bind. I have important information on a fraud case that could really—"

"Are you high?" the clerk asked, nonplussed.

"No, of cour—"

"Do you know it's Friday night?"

"Yes, of cour—"

"Then go away."

Okay, maybe charm was overrated.

Before Calla could figure out her next move, a heavyset uniformed officer appeared at the end of the hall.

Calla rushed toward him before anybody in the waiting room could move. "I need to see somebody in the fraud department!"

His gaze flicked over her with a hint of male interest before he rolled his eyes. "Lady, I got—"

"Please. It's an emergency."

"It always is." He sighed and pointed down the hall he'd just emerged from. "Sixth door on the left. See Detective Antonio."

"Thank you," Calla breathed, barely resisting the urge to kiss his pudgy cheek.

"Don!" the clerk shouted, leaping to her feet.

"What the hell you want me to do, Mary?" he hollered back. "I got an attempted murder to deal with here."

Calla barely heard the renewed wailing from the waiting room, she was too busy scooting down the hall.

The sixth door on the left had the pealing, fading letters of Detective Division printed on the smoked glass. Drawing a deep breath and hoping not everybody inside was as cranky as the front-desk clerk, Calla turned the handle.

The room she entered was scattered with several metal desks, each containing a computer monitor and various personal items. A water cooler and coffee station took up most of the space in the back, and directly across from her was a closed office door that read Lieutenant Meyer.

Except for the distant ringing of a phone, it was blessedly quiet.

Better yet, only two people were inside—a woman in a well-worn brown suit, who answered the phone, and a dark-haired man, typing rapidly on a keyboard.

She approached him, confident when she revealed her information, he'd be interested. Detectives moved up the ranks by solving cases, right? Certainly this one would be no exception.

Up close, she realized his hair wasn't brown but black—thick, wavy and slightly mussed, as if he'd raked his fingers through the locks repeatedly. His hands were large, and his broad shoulders strained against the confines of his wrinkled black shirt, the sleeves of which were rolled up to reveal darkly tanned and muscular forearms.

This was not a man to be messed with.

"Detective Antonio?" she asked, hating the tentative note in her voice.

After a few more strokes of the keyboard, he lifted his head. His face was handsome and sculpted but hard. His lips might have been full but were flattened at the moment with a scowl. Eyes, green as a shamrock, but imparting none of the cheeriness of Ireland's symbol, stared back at her with vivid reluctance.

"Yeah?" he returned, giving her a quick look from head to toe.

His expression didn't soften with the perusal, and she found herself struggling not to be insulted. Granted, it had been a long time since she'd been the Cotton Bowl Queen, but she generally got a spark of interest from most men.

She'd even had her hair highlighted and gotten a glowing spray tan the day before.

Like that matters. Get on with it, girl.

She held out her hand. "I'm Calla Tucker."

He rose, but not before expelling a tired sigh. "Devin Antonio," he said, wrapping his hand around hers.

Fire darted through Calla's body at the touch of his calloused palm. She flinched at the sensation and yanked her hand back, but it continued to tingle in the aftermath. He must have felt something similar since he glanced from her to his own hand and back again.

Now there was heat and anger in his remarkable eyes.

Though the tingling lingered, making her light-headed, she ignored it. She was supposed to be helping Shelby, not flirting.

"Devin," she said after clearing her throat. "That's an unusual name for an Italian."

His scowl deepened. "It's Irish. My mom was."

"Oh, I'm sorry. She passed away?"

"Hell if I know." He extended his hand to the chair opposite his desk. "Have a seat."

"Thank you," she said automatically, though her thoughts

were whirling. She'd traveled enough to know war and despair existed everywhere and on many different fronts. But even in abject poverty she'd seen families stick together and work hard to make the most of their circumstances.

She found it incredibly sad that Detective Antonio didn't know that kind of comfort.

"Reporters are supposed to stay in the press room," he said shortly.

"I'm not a reporter." She waved her hand. "Okay, I was at one time. I'm a features writer now. Mostly for travel and life-style magazines."

"And you're here to do a story on me." He glanced at his watch. "At seven o'clock on a Friday night?"

"No story, and why does everybody keep reminding me about the day and time? Writers work at all hours. Silly me, I thought the police station was pretty much a 24/7 seven operation."

"It is, but not for me. I was on my way out."

"You were typing."

"Finishing up a report. Are you in some kind of trouble, miss?"

"It's Calla, and, no, not me. It's my friend Shelby, specifically her parents."

Before he could interrupt or, worse, throw her back to the front-desk diva, Calla told him about how the Dixons had given their life savings to Max Banfield, only to see it go into his pocket.

"I've got statements from six other couples right here," she concluded, fishing in her briefcase for the folder containing the transcriptions she'd painstakingly documented from her recorded phone interviews. "They all implicate Maxwell Banfield as the head of the investment company."

The detective didn't even glance at the folder she laid on

his desk. "Investments come with a risk. I'm sure Mr. Banfield explained that to his clients."

"But he didn't even invest the money. Weeks after cashing the check, the phone number he gave was disconnected and the office abandoned."

"Fraud is a difficult case to prove."

"Then your job must be pretty damn miserable."

He stared directly at her. "It has its moments."

Was that his attempt to compliment her or was she one of the miserable moments? The guy was impossible to read.

"Look, miss, I—"

"Calla."

"Fine. Calla." He shoved her folder across the desk. "I've got ten open cases to work. And it looks like one of them is going to be transferred to Homicide, since the harbor patrol found my suspect floating in the East River about two hours ago."

She pushed the folder toward him. "Then you'll only have nine cases. You've got room for one more."

"No. I'll have to work with Homicide exclusively for the next few days, catching them up on all the background, which means I'll be even more backlogged once they take over."

Frustrated, Calla rose and turned away from him. Shelby and Victoria were right. The only way they were getting results was to get them on their own. She was wasting her time with the hot, angry detective.

"These statements aren't admissible in court," he said.

Calla turned. He'd opened her file. Suspicious of his curiosity, she nodded. "I know. I have the digital recordings to back up everything."

He shook his head. "Doesn't matter. All these people would have to be interviewed by a cop."

"So interview them." She glared down at him, feeling better that she had the height advantage. "You guys know something squirrelly's going on. Mrs. Rosenberg lives right here in the city, and she told me she filed a report with you guys months ago. Why won't you help?"

"The case crosses state lines. That makes it federal."

She leaned over, bracing her hand in the center of his desk. "Oh, that's just crap. Unless Banfield walks into a bank with a loaded pistol, it'll be years before the Feds get around to this case. And why should he resort to violence anyway? He's doing just fine, smiling and lying and taking every meager penny these hardworking people have spent their lives earning. It's unconscionable."

He stood, taking her advantage with a single movement. "Where the hell are you from?"

"Texas."

"That explains it." He raked his hand through his inky hair, just as she'd imagined earlier.

The state of attraction along with dissent was foreign to her. When she liked a guy, she liked him. She had no idea what to make of this encounter. Or of him and where he stood.

"I'm not supposed to tell you what I'm about to," he said, sounding as aggravated as he looked. "But I don't want you going all Wyatt Earp on me and shooting down the guy at the local watering hole."

"Wyatt Earp's showdown took place in Arizona, not Texas."

"You're sure?"

She crossed her arms over her chest. "Pretty positive. Not to mention that happened about 130 years ago. Texans are independent and self-sufficient, not idiotic."

"Stubborn comes to mind," he muttered. "But whatever. I actually know about Banfield. One of our guys interviewed Mrs. Rosenberg, but we couldn't find anybody else to corroborate her claim."

"That's because Banfield moves all over."

"He's technically a Brit. And now he's bought a hotel in midtown."

For the first time, Calla realized there was more going on behind the detective's emerald eyes than resentment. "He certainly has."

He tapped her folder with the tip of his finger. "I'll look into the statements of the other victims, though you should know that people are reluctant to go on record about being duped."

"I have complete faith in your powers of persuasion, Detective."

"I'll contact you if I have any questions. You got a card?"

She pulled one from the front pocket of her briefcase and handed it to him. "I appreciate you taking the time to see me."

His mouth twitched on one side, as if he might actually be tempted to smile. "All part of the community-service motto."

"Good to know."

She turned to leave without shaking his hand again. She finally felt as if they'd reached an even keel. The last thing she needed was to incite her lust again.

"And, Calla…"

When she turned, she found his perpetual scowl in place—which somehow didn't lessen his attractiveness. His toughness made him all the more appealing. "Hmm?" she asked, perfectly aware she was staring.

"We'd really rather keep our information to ourselves for now. Let me look into this. No more victim interviews. Don't go to the press. Don't approach Banfield, don't talk about him, don't contact him in any way. Clear?"

A picture of the party the night before flashed in Calla's memory. "Oh, sure." She swallowed. "I imagine the NYPD looks down on vigilantes."

"You bet your cute Texas ass we do."

5

"It was wonderful, Mario—truly." Shelby smiled warmly at the handsome Italian chef. "I'd love to know what you put in the marinara sauce."

Mario waggled his finger. "Not even for you, *bella.* My great-great grandmother would never let me past the gates of heaven."

"We can't let that happen. How about a trade? I'll bring you four dozen of my chocolate-chunk caramel cookies, and you give me four jars of that sauce?"

With a smile, Mario nodded. "This is an excellent idea."

They agreed to trade on Tuesday, and Shelby picked up her wineglass with a satisfied sigh. She might be in a financial and emotional pinch, but the best things in life were sometimes easy to come by.

She directed her attention to Trevor, wondering if, with his privileged upbringing, he'd taken that kind of thing for granted.

"How nice of you to notice I'm still here," he said, drumming his long, elegant fingers against the table.

Impulsively, she covered his hand with hers. "Sorry. I get carried away by great food. Occupational hazard."

He lifted her hand to his mouth, brushing his lips over her

fingers in an old-fashioned gesture that left her breathless. "I agree the food has always been delicious here, but I've never gotten such exceptional service." He paused, his expression wry. "But then Mario never seemed enamored with my cleavage."

"Oh, good grief. He's married and has four kids."

"Yes, well, I'm not so sure his wife would be impressed by his close customer service."

Trevor's possessiveness should have bothered her. It didn't. "You're jealous?"

"I like cookies, too."

Delighted and charmed, she squeezed his hand and scooted closer to him in the intimate corner booth they shared. "How many do you want?"

"If Mario gets four dozen, I want five."

"I could also add dark chocolate and cranberries to yours. It gives the sweet cookies a hint of tartness."

"I like tart and sweet."

"Then that's what you'll have."

She'd gone out with him to spy and help her parents' cause—or so she'd told herself at the start of the evening.

She should be probing Trevor for information about Max and wondering if he'd told her the truth about his brother. Or if he actually knew Max was an amoral creep. Or if he knew anything about this investor's meeting. But she'd barely given the Robin Hood matter a minute's thought. In fact, she'd purposely avoided the subject of Max, as the more she enjoyed time with Trevor, the more guilty she felt for misleading him about her true motives.

Dinner had been delightful. Trevor was intelligent and attentive. He was determined and self-made, despite counting royalty among his friends. His wit had its British moments, but since he'd left his family's long shadow and come to New York at the young age of twenty-two, his ideas had a distinctly

American slant. And maybe, most importantly, the idea of him sharing DNA with a scheming, self-absorbed creep like Max Banfield seemed ludicrous.

She wished she could convince herself she was impressed by him because her last decent date had been months ago, but she knew deep down that Trevor would be impressive to anyone and in any situation.

"Should I bring the cookies Tuesday?" she asked.

"How about right after you deliver Mario's? Then they'll be dessert after I take you to a great steak house. Have you ever eaten at Palo's?"

She had—once. Victoria had treated her and Calla after Victoria had landed an important client but lost her latest lover because she'd spent so much time wooing the big client.

Shelby, however, couldn't afford to order so much as a salad there at the moment. Her stomach clenched. Was she using him again? Had her dip into spying, eavesdropping and vindictiveness already shifted her morals?

No, she decided quickly. Not yet anyway. She'd go to dinner with Trevor if they ate at a hot-dog stand on the street corner. And surely she could keep her personal relationship with him separate from her revenge quest. The subject of Max would be off-limits. Easy as pie.

"I'd love to have dinner Tuesday," she said. "Especially at Palo's."

He brushed his lips over hers, like a whisper…or a promise. "So date number two is secured even before the end of date number one? And here I thought my previous kissing technique would hamper me."

"Your technique is fine."

"Just fine?"

"You kissing me didn't aggravate me at the time—only later, after I found out who you were."

"But the Banfield men have established a reputation for

charm. My great-grandfather had a constant stream of mistresses, supposedly reaching double digits, and my grandfather had four wives. My father's broken the mold by staying single since he and my mother divorced, but it's early days yet. He's not yet sixty."

She raised her eyebrows. "How many do you intend to have?"

"One. But then I'm exceedingly picky. Much like you with whom you allow to kiss you."

"Sorry to be difficult. There are a lot of players in this city—and not only the kind in sports."

His gaze searched her face. "You think I'm playing you?"

No. Um, probably not. Besides, in light of her current agenda, she could hardly demand full disclosure from him. "Maybe we should try it again. The kissing, I mean, just to see if last night was a fluke."

"I look forward to the challenge."

The desire and promise in his beautiful blue eyes made her dizzy with heat. *Why me?* she nearly asked. He could have anyone—and probably had. Given his secrecy the night before, she wondered if she was trusting too easily and falling too quickly.

Yet logic dictated an unarguable fact—if Max had sent his brother out to romance women for his latest scheme, most notably the mysterious investors' meeting, he would have certainly picked Victoria. The suit she'd been wearing during the party had been Chanel, and a man as sophisticated as Trevor could certainly spot that kind of quality next to Shelby's serviceable black pants she'd bought on sale at The Gap.

Maybe he simply had a thing for redheads.

Regardless, she needed to stop overthinking every move and enjoy herself. She couldn't possibly hold Nearly Royal Trevor's interest for long.

The waitress arrived and cleared their plates, suggesting

Mario's coveted tiramisu for dessert, which they agreed to share.

When they were alone again, Trevor slid his hand down Shelby's back in a casual gesture that suggested he'd done it a million times before. He was clearly a tactile kind of person, reminding her of men in her native Georgia. The idea comforted, as she'd gotten used to more reserved New Yorkers. She'd learned years ago not to hug people unexpectedly the way everyone did down South.

"I was serious last night at Max's party, by the way," he said.

Max's name had her fighting a jolt.

Okay, so maybe not easy as pie, separating revenge and romance. It might be more like soufflé—lots of broken eggs and fervent prayers that the finished product wouldn't collapse.

Stalling, she sipped her wine. "Really? About what?"

"The dinner party I'd like to plan."

Relief washed through her. "Oh, right."

He angled his head, studying her. "You don't mind discussing business over dessert, do you?"

"No." She smiled, hoping to cover her brief discomfort. "I do my best work surrounded by food."

Enjoying cappuccino with their tiramisu, they discussed the details of a party he wanted to host for a potential new client and his top executives. He emphasized elegance, but nothing stuffy. His would-be clients were running a company started by their proud-to-be-blue-collar grandfather and enjoyed muscle cars and rye whiskey more than limos and fine wine.

Shelby suggested a steak and potatoes meal, plus a light salad tossed tableside. The meat would be acquired from her prime supplier and butter and cheese always made a popular accompaniment to any kind of potato.

Trevor agreed simplicity was best and told her his apartment address. She couldn't swallow her gasp fast enough.

"I did mention my business was fairly lucrative, didn't I?" he asked smoothly.

Actually, he hadn't. And even though Calla's article had given her a fair idea of his success, the reminder of the difference in their lifestyles was shoved into the brightness of reality.

"I figured you worked hard," she managed to say.

"So do you."

"Caterers don't make what transportation moguls do."

Laughing, he slid his arm around her waist, holding her to his side. "And yet we're all outpaced by guys who can throw a football sixty yards. It's a strange world sometimes."

After the check was presented, paid and whisked away, Trevor led her outside to a waiting cab.

"I'm surprised you don't have a limo and driver."

"I like being a regular New Yorker." He linked his fingers with hers, letting their joined hands rest on the worn black vinyl seat. "I especially don't like people waiting on me every minute of the day."

"I would have imagined you'd be used to that."

"No. As I said earlier, I'm the second son. My safety, education and general health was taken care of. But as for anything else, I was pretty much on my own."

"On your…" The coldness of his words hit her, even though he communicated no resentment. "Your parents?"

"My parents divorced—rather bitterly—when I was five. My father was busy with parliament. My mother became obsessed with screwing every tennis instructor in England. My father booted her off the estate when he found out, though I expect the abruptness had more to do with the gossip than unfaithfulness. I've always wondered if he still pines for her, no matter how inappropriate she was for him and his proper life, but instead of women, Dad focused all his energy in molding the perfect heir." With a crooked smile, he shrugged. "Everybody copes with setbacks in their own way."

So Trevor was ignored in favor of *Max?* Shelby could barely contain her outrage. "But—"

"Being on my own taught me self-reliance. I've never had Max's obligations to the future title, never wanted them. Never had to live up to anything but my own expectations, as long as I did everything my father asked, of course." Regret filled his eyes. "The divorce hit Max harder than me. He was devoted to Mum, while I had Florence, who was my governess back then."

In other words, she was the only one who cared, Shelby thought.

He stroked her cheek. "Your face is turning as red as your hair. Don't be outraged for me. Remember, I'm related to George the Third—yes, the one who fought the American colonists. I have an excellent pedigree."

She stared at him in disbelief. "Who cares about that?"

He pressed his lips against her skin. "A great many people."

His breath stirred her hair; his scent stirred her senses. Maybe her allure wasn't the color of her hair after all. Maybe he liked her simply because she was normal.

Since his upbringing certainly wasn't familiar. At least to her.

And all she'd done lately was complain about the burden of her parents. While not living up to Daddy's expectations certainly didn't excuse Max's swindling schemes, Trevor's devotion to his family, flaws and all, was humbling.

She laid her palm against his chest, feeling the strong, sure beat of his heart. "Why aren't you angry?"

"Because they're family. No matter our differences, I can't unchoose them the way I can select my friends. And besides the posturing and rules and general silliness, the Banfields have been part of English society for hundreds of years. I have a responsibility to honor them as best I can. I imagine you'd do anything for your family."

Dropping her gaze, Shelby nodded. She was doing something for her family, all right.

The cab pulled to a halt in front of the cozy, Chelsea-area redbrick apartment building where Shelby lived. The streetlights illuminated the generous sprinkling of shady trees as well as the front-porch pots filled with bright spring flowers. It was a dream to live there.

Shelby's landlady was rich as a queen and charged her renters a modest monthly sum. Thankfully, she'd hired Shelby to cater her birthday party three years ago and fell in love with Shelby's chicken cacciatore. She'd quickly become one of Mrs. Hines's beneficiaries, which had allowed her to move out of Brooklyn and into the city.

Trevor paid the cabdriver, then he walked Shelby to the door. "Business must be pretty decent," he said, his gaze roving the building.

"I do okay." She explained about Mrs. Hines. "As long as my tomato supplier doesn't bug out on me, and I make her a spectacular birthday cake every year, it's like having rent control."

"It's a great area. We're nearly neighbors. I live on 26th, remember?"

He probably *owned* 26th, but at least Shelby could be proud to show him her place. Very few people in her income bracket could afford to live so well. "You want to come up for coffee?"

"I very much want to come up. But not for coffee." He slid his arm around her waist and cupped her jaw in his palm. "I should probably go."

Belying his suggestion, his mouth covered hers with assurance, his tongue sliding between her lips in a teasing invitation that she felt to her toes. She leaned against him, feeling his muscle tone and the heat of his body through his pristine white shirt.

Desire, hot and sweet, invaded her as it hadn't in a long, long time.

Or at least since last night anyway.

Everything about him called to her. She wanted to know if he'd been as scared to leave all he'd known in England, just as she'd been both terrified and excited to move away from her childhood home. She wondered if his father's indifference had spurred him to the great success he'd clearly achieved. She longed to know everything from his views on politics to his favorite music and foods.

She wrapped her arms around his neck and held him against her. The kiss went on with their hearts racing in sync and long, drugging sensations that seduced her more thoroughly than she'd ever known.

"Well?" he asked, pulling back.

Hazy from the sweet sensation of his kiss, Shelby fought to remember where she was—other than in his arms—what year it was or what planet she inhabited. Her gaze focused on his mouth as she wondered when she could have it on hers again. "Hmm?"

"Technique, my lady."

"Oh." She blinked. "Right. Yes, well…" She cleared her throat and prayed her brain would communicate something intelligible to her mouth. "Excellent work, your Lordship."

"Glad to hear it. Men do have an ego where these things are concerned."

"Yeah?" She blinked dazedly, as the look in his eyes wasn't ego, but hunger. "Yours should be secure, then."

"It'll hold till Tuesday." He pressed his lips to hers one last time, then started down the steps. At the bottom, he turned. "Are you sure you don't have a thing for titles? I wasn't kidding when I said I don't have one."

"Me, either. You started it with the *my lady* business." Noting he was frowning and realizing this was a hot-button issue for him, she added, "Frankly, I don't have a clue how the English aristocracy works, and the only title I have a thing for is *chef.* Good enough?"

His smile sent a renewed buzz through her body. "It's certainly a promising start."

He walked down the street, and she watched him until his tall silhouette faded into the night.

She was fairly certain she'd fallen into a fairy tale. Hadn't Victoria said Robin Hood was a myth when they'd started on this crazy project? By agreeing to the plan had she somehow challenged the time-space continuum and blurred the lines between fantasy and reality?

"No," she muttered to herself, unlocking the door. "But you've certainly been watching too many late-night movies on the SciFi channel."

Despite the fact that Trevor was related to the man she'd targeted for revenge, the attraction was enticing and exciting. Why shouldn't she pursue it?

Because, other than hot kisses and family trials, he's as out of your league as the aliens in the movie you watched last Friday night.

Her practical voice also reminded her she was inching toward the unethical side of the line. Hell, if she turned around she'd probably see the line behind her.

But all she could think about was how to get closer to Trevor.

6

"BOUNCED!" SHELBY SHOUTED, slapping the offending, worthless check on the prep counter. "The man is a menace."

"I can't imagine why you're surprised," Victoria commented, flipping through a fashion magazine. "The guy's an idiot."

"He has a certain amount of charm," Calla said.

Victoria shook her head. *"Please."*

"Surely you recall that he's lured a lot of people into giving him their life savings," Calla argued.

"Not any people I know."

"Oh, right. You're infallible. Maybe you should sell savvy lessons." Calla smiled with mock sweetness. "Then again... that last client of yours and his organic toothpaste were both horrible."

Victoria slapped her magazine closed. "It was not. And what does that have to do with Max Banfield?"

From years of practice, Shelby tuned out her friends' bickering. It was like being caught at a tennis match between Pollyanna and Darth Vader.

Her thoughts instead turned to Max's upcoming investors' meeting. Neither Victoria nor Calla had been able to get a lead on when, where or specifically what the meeting was being organized for. Max was either very selective about his invitees, or he'd simply been bragging at the party, and the meeting was a myth.

Trevor would know.

They were due to have dinner that night. She'd asked her friends to meet her in her kitchen because she was frantically baking cookies for both him and Mario, the Italian chef Trevor had accused of flirting with her on their Friday-night date.

She and Trevor had talked and texted several times since then. While she'd worked three events over the weekend, he'd spent the time at his house in the Hamptons. For some reason, the dichotomy didn't bother her. But then she was currently involved in a delusion involving a mythical vigilante, so her judgment was shaky at best.

She'd gotten a stunning bouquet of flowers that morning. Trevor had admitted in the note that his secretary—aka Florence, the former governess—had picked them out, as he'd been in Boston since Monday morning.

So honest.

She'd prided herself on the same. At least she had a couple of weeks ago.

Now she was caught between what she needed and what was right. And that revelation went straight back to her plan to ruin Max. Was she getting justice, or was she unjustifiably vengeful? In her investigation, would she hurt those who were innocent? Should she be patient and hope the authorities would make him pay?

Eventually, anyway.

No easy answers. Like the most challenging of life's fights, not everybody could win, not everybody would be satisfied with the battle plan. Not all the lieutenants…

She whirled to her friends. "His assistant would know about the meeting."

Her friends stopped long enough to drag themselves from their debate and gave her identically confused looks. "Who's assistant?" Calla asked.

"Max's." The oven timer beeped, so Shelby retrieved the last batch of cookies. "Somebody's fielding calls, sending out invites and booking a conference room."

"He could be doing all that himself," Victoria said, though she looked speculative. "He could be holding the meeting in his own hotel."

"You really think Max is doing his own paperwork?" Calla asked, clearly doubtful.

"Exactly." Shelby ripped off her oven mitt and approached the kitchen's center island where her friends had gathered. "So there's a secretary, assistant or clerk who knows what's going on. We just have to get to her."

"Or him," Calla said.

"Her," Victoria insisted. "You really think Max is evolved enough to have a male assistant?"

"He has an office somewhere," Shelby said, hoping to head off another skirmish. "Let's find out where. Did either of you get his card?"

Victoria nodded. "I did, but no address. Just a phone and email."

"We could ask sexy Detective Antonio," Calla said.

"I don't care how sexy he is," Victoria said, raising her eyebrows. "Which you've reminded us of at least four times in the last hour, by the way. The last thing we need is a New York City cop catching wind of what we're doing."

They hadn't really done anything. Not yet.

Except lie, her conscience reminded her brutally.

"Max's card is a place to start." Shelby paced beside the counter. "What're we going to do when we find the address, though? March in and demand the assistant hand over the investors' information?"

"Maybe your boyfriend can help us out," Victoria said drily.

Shelby shook her head. "Trevor is far from my boyfriend, and I'm not getting him involved in this, regardless."

"Why not?" Victoria asked.

Shelby knew her excuse would sound lame, but she was going for it anyway. "I'm keeping him and Max separate."

"Separate?" Calla echoed, sounding doubtful.

"Does the phrase *sleeping with the enemy* ring any bells?" Victoria asked, typically blunt.

Shelby shook her head. "I'm not sleeping with him."

"Not yet," Victoria said.

"Trevor doesn't have anything to do with Max's schemes," Shelby insisted, transferring the cookies to a cooling rack.

Victoria swiped a warm cookie from the pan. "And you know that due to his good looks and slick, flirty smile?"

"Stop already," Calla said. "I happen to agree with Shelby." Before Victoria could follow through with another reality check, she added, "Which I base on hard evidence. He's loaded because of legitimate means. Why would he need a shady scheme?"

Victoria shrugged. "Some people do it for the thrill."

Calla narrowed her eyes. "Now you're being deliberately difficult."

With obvious joy, Victoria contemplated another bite of her cookie. "When am I ever easy?"

Calla and Shelby exchanged commiserating looks. Despite Victoria's healthy bank account and in-crowd business connections, she had plenty of issues to deal with. Her drive to succeed was a living, breathing, often invincible force that ruled her life.

Calla slipped her arm around Victoria's shoulders. "Never. It's part of your charm."

Smiling, Shelby moved the cooled cookies to a pastry box. "You know we're grateful for your honesty."

"We could all use a bit of bluntness at the moment," Calla added.

"Fine," Victoria said. "Ask Trevor about the investors' meeting."

Shelby closed the box. "He doesn't know anything."

Victoria leaned toward her. "Bet he does."

On the other side of the counter, Shelby mirrored her pose. "Bet what?"

Victoria brandished the remains of her chocolate-infused cookie. "My own dozen of these."

"What do I get if I win?" Shelby asked, wondering if she should patent the recipe, since it was such an obvious hit.

"The information about the investors' meeting."

Not a bad trade, really. Shelby would show her cynical friend that Trevor was one of the rare good guys. "Deal."

Victoria's only response was a triumphant smile as she polished off the last of the cookie.

Shelby had loaded her pastry boxes into the catering company's logo tote bags—one for Mario, one for Trevor—when complete comprehension over her agreement hit home.

She'd been goaded into asking Trevor about his brother.

"What have I done?" she wondered aloud as she sank against the counter.

"Remembered that you're supposed to be helping us help you help your parents," Victoria said calmly.

Shelby glanced around her kitchen, her pride and joy, the heart and soul of her business. If she had to sell everything and go home to take care of her parents, this would be nothing but a memory. Sure, she could start over in Savannah, but how many years would it take to claw her way back to the moderate success she'd worked and sacrificed to gain in New York? What would she tell her employees, many of whom had been with her since the beginning?

And even if that potential nightmare didn't worry her, the idea of partitioning Max and Trevor into separate areas of her life seemed lame and most likely futile. Making Max pay was only going to come about through clever plans, total dedication and a whole lot of luck.

If she wasn't very, very careful, though, she wasn't only going to break a few eggs, she was going to burn them to ash.

Victoria gave Calla a sage look. "She's more worried about upsetting Trevor than getting revenge on Max."

Shelby straightened. "I am not."

Though, admittedly, she was looking forward to seeing Trevor so much, she'd been preoccupied enough to reach for cinnamon instead of cayenne pepper when making jambalaya that morning.

"So you'll ask him about the meeting," Victoria insisted.

Sighing, Shelby reluctantly nodded. "Fine."

She wondered if she should ruin her date before or after she got her sixty-dollar steak.

A FEW HOURS LATER, SHELBY set down her fork with a different kind of sigh. "That was the most amazing steak I've ever eaten."

Staring at her over the rim of his wineglass, Trevor's dreamy blue eyes glowed. "It was a pleasure to watch you eat it."

Shelby cocked her head. "You're not some kind of weirdo who gets off watching women chew, are you?"

"No." He laughed. "Is there an epidemic of that kind of guy?"

"In this city, you never know."

"Yes, I suppose that's true. I'm simply glad we're compatible in our culinary interests. A lot of women these days eat nothing but salad."

"Not me. I'd rather run on the treadmill regularly and eat well."

"Me, too."

He was just so damn likable, agreeable, as well as gorgeous. Plus, for a caterer, if the guy wasn't into food, then automatically there was going to be a problem.

You mean, other than the fact that you're about to tell a big fat lie to further your own agenda at the expense of his family?

"Speaking of eating well…" she began, dismissing her conscience like a switch of a light. "I've ordered everything for your dinner party on Friday. I got a beautiful tenderloin. I could cut it into filets, but I was thinking about doing something more old-school. How do you feel about Beef Wellington?"

"As in the Duke at Waterloo?"

"That's the one. At first I thought the paté and puff pastry were too fussy, but you can cut the dish at the table, which makes things more homey. Even a manly man kind of thing."

"A manly man kind of thing," he repeated, looking confused.

"Yeah, you know, like a *Release the hounds!* bonding experience. Didn't you tell me these clients of yours have a hunting lodge in Ohio?"

"They do." He smiled suddenly, brushing his lips across her cheek and sending her pulse into overdrive. "Brilliant. They'll love it. You've thought of everything."

"That's what I get paid for. You're my client, so my goal is to make the clients happy. Speaking of clients… Do you have any idea what's involved in this investors' meeting of Max's?"

Trevor blinked. Complete bafflement suffused his face for several seconds. "Investors'… Max? My brother Max?"

"Right. Another great client." She decided against mentioning the bounced check. "He told Victoria about some kind of meeting for an investment project, but they got separated during the party, and she never heard all the details. She asked me if I'd talk to you, see if you knew what was going on."

Not a lie. Well, not all of it anyway.

Trevor said nothing, merely linking his fingers, then lightly resting his chin on them. It was a precisely choreographed pose—Central Casting's version of Deep in Thought.

His reaction made Shelby's mouth go dry. *He knows something.*

"Hmm," he murmured. "That's odd. He never mentioned this to me."

"Does he usually?"

"He invests in various projects." Trevor chuckled but Shelby could hear the tension underlying the humor. "Much more adventurous than I am, certainly."

"That's strange. Victoria's pretty conservative."

"But she's wealthy."

There seemed little point in denying the obvious. Trevor had had ample time to discover who Victoria was, but had he taken the time? Maybe this was some kind of test of Shelby's honesty?

Which you'd fail, by the way.

Shelby nodded. "Her last name is Holmes, as in the Holmes Cardiac Wing at Midtown Memorial. As in Wyforth, Holmes and Stein, law firm to the stars."

Trevor's mouth tightened. "I see."

"Do you think your brother's next project is really risky?"

Trevor's expression instantly cleared. "I'm sure it's fine. Would you like me to ask Max about it?"

"Thanks, that would be great."

He linked his hand with hers. "For you, anything."

The warmth of his touch chased away the sharp edge of her doubt. She was getting paranoid, imposing her own troubles and uncertainties on his reactions. She'd asked; he'd answered. Was she supposed to interrogate the man? They barely knew each other. Maybe he did share secrets with his brother. She couldn't possibly expect to be privy to them all.

As they shared coffee and dessert of a rich and dark chocolate mousse, Shelby told him about her first attempt to make mousse for a family gathering, which was a complete disaster, top to bottom.

"Making truly great mousse requires considerable skill, doesn't it? How old were you?"

"Eight."

He coughed. "That's awfully young. You didn't ask your mother for help?"

"No way. Mom can't cook anything that doesn't come from a microwaveable box. My grandmother taught me. She was a great cook."

"Was?"

"She died three years ago." And, boy, could Shelby have used her advice at the moment. Granny would have known what to do about this swindling business. Though, given her fiery nature, she likely would have approved of the *any means necessary* avenue for justice. "She had a stroke playing the back nine of her favorite golf course."

"I'm sorry," Trevor said gently.

Shelby smiled. "She's probably still ticked off. Her score card showed she was on track to hit par."

"My father and his friends are obsessed with golf, as well. But then he has no culinary taste, much less skill, so he hardly compares to your grandmother. His favorite meal is well-done roast beef and boiled potatoes."

"Roast is comfort food," Shelby said neutrally. "I imagine it's stressful to be an earl."

"I doubt it's all that taxing. And he dictated roast three to five days a week. Probably still does. He likes predictability."

"And you don't?"

Leaning close, Trevor laid his hand on her thigh. "I like surprises."

Oh, good. You'll be thrilled when you discover I'm a big fat liar.

Shelby ignored the warning. Instead, she angled her body toward Trevor. The heat of his hand was separated from her skin only by her dress's thin, clingy fabric.

The fact that they were introduced through subterfuge was a vague worry. Desire hung between them, an impulse unfulfilled.

As yet.

Though his gaze dropped briefly to her lips, he continued. "The crazy thing was at Westmore Manor we had—"

"Westmore Manor. Seriously, your childhood home has a name?"

"The entire property has its own postal code. Is that helpful?"

"Not in the least."

He wrapped his arm around her waist. "I'm trying to compliment you, would you like to hear how?"

"Oh, please continue."

"At Westmore Manor…" He cast a glance at her, and she mockingly rolled her eyes. "We had an actual chef in charge of the kitchen. A highly accomplished French chef. He wanted to make Coquilles Saint-Jacques, Brie tarts and escargot with mushrooms."

"And your father wanted beef and potatoes."

"Chef Frances, carrying his German-made knives, ran cursing from the house one night during dinner when I was fourteen." Trevor's eyes lit with the memory. "But before that, I used to sneak down to his kitchen and try the food he *wanted* to cook. He had such passion. Passion my father was apparently determined to stamp out."

Shelby watched the shadow fall over his face. "Like with you."

"Not exactly. He wanted to control, more than omit." His expression cleared, the charm she'd become accustomed to reasserting. "But I didn't suffer for the challenges I've faced. Neither, I expect, has Chef Frances, since he now owns one of the most accomplished and prestigious restaurants in London."

"One you financed."

His eyes registered shock.

She flushed, self-conscious by her blurted response. "Just a hunch."

"You're a continual surprise—another compliment. The original one was that you remind me of Chef Frances." He trailed his fingers across her cheek. "Full of energy and passion."

She leaned into his caress. "A rarity in Westmore Manor?"

His smile flashed. "Not for everyone."

The man was amazing. Clever. Desirable. Interesting. What more did she need?

From the depths of her purse, Shelby heard her phone buzz, indicating a text message had come through. Wincing, she leaned away from Trevor. "Sorry. Do you mind if I check that? I have a big luncheon to cater tomorrow, and the hostess keeps adding to the guest list."

Gracious as always, Trevor said, "Go ahead. I have some difficult clients myself."

When Shelby pulled out her phone, she noticed the text was from Calla. She started to ignore it, then saw the beginning, Never mind asking T...

She clicked on the message. In full it read, Never mind asking Trevor. We're going to break into Max's office instead.

Oh, goody. Shelby the Caterer and her gleeful, oh-so-passionate band of vigilantes seemed destined for the slammer.

"What are you up to?" Trevor demanded as he strode into Max's office the next morning.

Seemingly unfazed by Trevor's abrupt entrance, Max leaned back in his black leather executive chair. "Good afternoon to you, too."

Trevor braced his hands on Max's desk. "Investors' meeting. Ring any bells?"

"I hold lots of meetings. I'm a busy man."

"And an evasive one."

"I don't answer to you."

"I'll remember that the next time you invest in hot-air-balloon rides."

Something was definitely going on with Max. Trevor knew by now that strong-arm tactics would get him nowhere with his brother. However, the idea of Max using one of Shelby's friends, and the consequences that might ensue, had affected his judgment.

Reaching deeply for his usual control, he lowered himself into a wide leather chair opposite Max. His brother's business address was fairly shabby, but he'd made himself and his guests comfortable in furnishings. "If you needed investors, you could have come to me."

"It's a small project. Nothing you'd be interested in."

"Try me."

Max expelled a long-suffering sigh. "Real estate. It's a real-estate investment."

"Where?"

"Downtown. A loft in the East Village. An artist died, and

his grandmother, who owned the building, wants me to find a contractor to divide the property into condos, then sell them."

Great day. Max knew less about contractors and real estate than he did about hotel ownership. His tendency was for poker and roulette. How he'd have better luck at a game that involved actual skill and judgment, Trevor couldn't imagine. "So the investors are for condos?"

"Yes."

"It seems awfully early in the process to be looking for buyers."

"The building is in a very desirable location."

"So you're going to get them to invest in a condo that isn't even built yet."

"It's done all the time."

"With established developers perhaps." Frustrated, Trevor rose and wandered around the office, full of books, artful lighting, polished cherry furniture, the latest electronics. A facade of a workspace. Like Max himself. "Who's going to build the condos?"

"I haven't decided. I'm taking bids."

"Don't you think owning a hotel and developing East Village condos are a bit too much to take on at the same time?"

Max's expression became petulant. "You handle multiple projects. Why shouldn't I?"

"Because you tend to lose interest rather quickly. Both hotel ownership and contracting involve commitment for more than a couple of weeks. How's your new girlfriend by the way?"

The abrupt switch in topic caused Max's left hand to jerk. He tried to cover the move by linking his fingers, as if that had been his intention all along. "Great. We're spending the weekend in the Hamptons."

"What's her name?"

"Julie. She's delicate, and needs me. She had a recent tragedy."

A horrible, but near certain, idea occurred to Trevor. "She wouldn't happen to be the former lover of a downtown artist, whose grandmother has just inherited a building?"

Red spots suffused Max's cheeks. "Now that you mention it…"

Trevor's stomach turned. The artist's body probably wasn't yet cold. And what had Max, and the fickle girlfriend, said to his grandmother to get her to agree to the condo development?

This was a step down—way down—from ill-advised, bordering-on-ridiculous business deals, from running up tabs in pubs and losing cash he didn't have to Vegas casinos. This was sleazy. Maybe Trevor should have expected his brother's continual downfall. Maybe he should have sent him home when he'd shown up in New York two years ago, claiming he wanted a fresh start. Maybe he and his father should have actually cut him off, instead of continuing to quietly bail him out. Though he'd hoped Max would see the futility of the path he was traveling, another part worried he was too far down the road to find his way back.

Still, Trevor's responsibility to his family legacy loomed. Max was the future of the Banfields, however much they were all concerned about what would happen when he eventually got his hands on the jeweled coffers.

"Deals like this are made all the time from inside sources," Max said, his tone defensive.

"Yes, I'm sure they are. Why should grief and ethics get in the way of making a buck?"

"Easy for you to say—you have a lot of bucks."

"I earned them."

"I'm entitled to them."

Angry by the almost comical twist of fate that had given his father an irresponsible heir and a dependable—though superfluous—second son, Trevor clenched his fist. He truly didn't want the title. Not that he could have it, even if wishing would make it so. The guilt over the fact that he didn't want Max's burden was no doubt what made him desperate for his brother to make a success of his life.

He and his father were bailing water out of a leaking lifeboat, though no amount of speed seemed capable of keeping the dream vessel afloat.

"How are bookings at the hotel?" he asked his brother, facing him with a smile and hoping to diffuse the tense atmosphere.

"Okay, I guess. I haven't talked to my manager in the last few days."

Like a toddler with a shiny new toy, Max was already bored with his. The only question now seemed to be which financial misstep would be the first to cause him to fall.

"You might want to check in with him," Trevor said as he moved toward the door.

"Yeah, I was just about to do that."

Trevor had his hand on the knob when Max called after him, "Do you know any contractors you can introduce me to?"

Over the years, Trevor had placated, enabled, tried the buddy system and bailouts. Nothing seemed to get through Max's unrealistic expectations. Florence wanted Trevor to push the baby bird from the nest. Time for some tough love.

And yet he could hardly refuse such a simple request.

"I'll send you some names. When is the investors' meeting?"

"Next Thursday at seven. Suite 1634 at the Crown."

Trevor suppressed a jolt. "That's fast."

"I need to judge interest before I start construction."

He needs money before he starts construction. "Of course you do." Trevor met Max's gaze with a glare. "If you embarrass this family again, I'm finished defending you."

Max frowned. "Since when have I embarrassed anybody?"

Trevor dearly hoped delusional tendencies weren't contagious. Especially since he was pretty sure they were hereditary.

7

Project Robin Hood, Day Eleven
The Campbell Building

"I CAN'T BELIEVE WE'RE doing this," Shelby said, staring out
her van's windshield at the dimly lit back door of the building
where Max Banfield rented his business office.

The differences between him and his brother were apparent not only in appearance, intelligence and integrity, but also
success. The brick on the small midtown building was a dingy
gray and sandwiched between a sketchy looking Chinese restaurant and a twenty-four-hour gym.

Of course, if Max rented in a luxury high-rise, they
wouldn't have a prayer of breaking in, either.

"It's not like we're going to steal anything," Victoria said
matter-of-factly.

"Actually, we are," Calla reminded them from the backseat.
"We're stealing information."

"Should be no problem for a gang of criminals like us,"
Shelby commented sarcastically.

"We're not criminals," Victoria said.

Calla leaned forward. "Nor a gang."

Shelby was pretty sure those excuses wouldn't go over well

with the arraignment judge. "Before your mood-killing text, I was having a really nice time the other night," she said, pulling on a pair of fleece gloves, which Victoria insisted they needed so they wouldn't leave fingerprints.

Victoria glared at her. "So sorry we interrupted you getting laid."

Shelby stared right back. "I've got several pieces of my life hanging by a thread, so a little compassion wouldn't be out of place."

Calla exchanged a look with Victoria. "Clearly, she could use the sex."

Victoria pulled her own set of gloves from her handbag. "She and the hot Brit can pick up right where they left off… after we find out the details of the investors'— Duck!"

Shelby's head and Calla's nearly collided as they dived toward the center console. Just over the dashboard, Shelby saw a broad-shouldered guy carrying a huge canvas bag as he exited the gym beside the office building. "That was close," she whispered as the guy ambled down the street.

"Who works out at ten o'clock on a Thursday night?" Victoria opened the passenger's side door. "Come on. I'd rather not explain to some muscled gym rat just how innocent we are."

Using the security key card Calla had procured that morning by flirting with a lawyer who also rented in the building, the women slipped inside via the back door.

With no security cameras to worry about, Shelby tried to convince her racing heart they weren't in danger. In response, it ignored her reassurance and kept right on pounding.

"According to Calla's lawyer friend, Max's office is on the third floor," Victoria said as she moved down the hall. "Let's find the stairs."

"Why?" Shelby asked.

Victoria pushed open the stairwell entrance, took a quick

peek inside, then held open the door for the others. "Less chance of somebody seeing us."

"That's good planning," Shelby said.

"I went out with an FBI agent once." Victoria started up the stairs. "You learn things."

Calla fell into step beside Shelby. "Speaking of guys and learning, do you really think Detective Antonio was coming on to me?"

Victoria nodded. "With that *you bet your cute Texas ass* line? Definitely."

Shelby glanced at Calla. "You want to talk about your crush on the cop now? While we're in the middle of a B&E?"

"We talked about your sex life in the van," Calla returned. "And I don't have a crush on him."

"You haven't stopped talking about him for the last week," Victoria said.

Calla smiled. "Did I mention how sexy he was?"

"Several times," Shelby and Victoria said together.

"Still, he's awfully angry…" Reaching the landing, Calla started to tug open the third-floor door.

Victoria laid her hand over Calla's. "And a cop."

With a wince, Shelby joined them. "Considering what we're doing here, don't you think you should keep your distance from him, Calla?"

"That's some kind of advice, coming from you," Calla retorted, planting her hands on her hips. "You're practically in bed with our target's brother."

"Yeah." Shelby considered the benefits of being in bed with Trevor and quickly decided the risk was worth the experience—should she ever be offered the opportunity. "A valid point there."

Victoria cracked open the door. "Later, girls. Save the relationship chat for after our successful mission."

"Mission?" Calla angled her head. "Just how long did you date the FBI guy?"

Victoria didn't answer. She craned her neck around the door, presumably to check to see if the coast was clear. Which it must have been, since she waved Shelby and Calla into the hall behind her. "When we get into the office, Shelby will search Max's desk, Calla will—"

"How are we getting into the office?" Calla asked.

"How else?" Victoria answered. "My credit card."

"That only works in the movies," Calla said.

Victoria pulled her black Am Ex from her jacket pocket. "Nobody turns this baby down."

Bringing up the rear of the group, Shelby glanced behind her, certain she'd heard footsteps. The hallway was empty. Clearly, she wasn't cut out for criminal life. She increased her pace to stride beside Victoria. "I don't care how we get in, let's just get in."

They reached the office with Max's name on the door, and Victoria, her hand steady as a surgeon's, slid her credit card between the frame and the locking bolt. Like magic, the door popped open.

While Calla appeared astounded, Shelby poked her friends in their lower backs to get them moving inside. Closing the door behind her, she leaned against it.

The office consisted of a small reception area, some fake potted ficus trees and a modest oak desk for an assistant. The open doorway across the room led to a spacious office holding a black marble desk, black leather chairs and bookcases. Shelby could also see the edge of a leopard-print couch.

Predictably tacky, but plush.

But was Max really a master criminal? Maybe he'd gotten in over his head with a business deal, panicked and used the retirement project money—belonging to her parents and others—to cover his losses. Was she overreacting? Had she drawn her friends, as well as her potential lover, into a desperate mix-up?

Of course, he'd also evaded the police, lied, skipped town and denied any wrongdoing. He hadn't stood up for his mistakes. He'd run from them.

She fisted her hands at her sides. "Victoria, you search Max's office. Calla, look around the secretary's desk. I'll stand guard."

"Why am I searching?" Victoria asked.

"I'm...nervous." Shelby's hand twitched as evidence. She clenched her fist tighter. "Can we please do this?" She swore she heard the elevator jolting into movement. "You know, quickly?"

Her friends, bless them, said nothing and headed off to their assigned duties. Shelby pressed her ear to the door. *Silence.*

Great. They were going to get through this.

Everything was going to be fine. She was going to get Max on some kind of illegal activity. She was going to get her parents' retirement money back. She was going to get her lover's—well, *potential* lover's—brother arrested.

How—

The doorknob beside her hip rattled, then the door flew open, propelling her forward. She caught herself on the corner of the secretary's desk.

Whirling, she came face-to-face with the reason.

A black-haired, green-eyed, broad-shouldered man filled the doorway. Armed man, she corrected silently when her gaze zoned in on the pistol strapped to his side.

Well, hell. Detective Antonio.

His gaze cut past Shelby to Calla. "What the hell are you doing, Ms. Tucker?"

Victoria slid into the door opening opposite the cop. "Well, Calla," she said in a breathy tone, "for once you weren't exaggerating."

The detective was sexy all right. But he was dangerous. And not just because he undoubtedly had handcuffs and a badge in the pocket of his leather jacket. Furious heat rolled off him in waves, yet when those vivid eyes focused on Calla's face, the anger turned to hunger.

And not the kind Shelby satisfied with seafood au gratin.

He took two forceful steps inside the office, flicking the door closed behind him with the toe of his shoe. "Have you lost your hearing *and* your mind?" he asked, clearly directing his attention to Calla.

Though he wasn't anything like the guys Calla usually went for, Shelby distinctly heard her friend let out a needy sigh. "I'm great," she said, her face flushed an aroused pink.

The detective's response was to cross his arms over his chest while he continued to stare at Calla with both fascination and expectation.

Shelby glanced at Victoria, who shrugged.

Then, like a switch had been flicked on, Calla blinked. She glowered at the detective. "What I'm doing here is none of your business. What are *you* doing here?"

"Keeping you—" his gaze swept over Victoria and Shelby "—and your gang from committing a felony."

"We're not a gang," Shelby said, echoing Calla's earlier assertion.

"And we're not committing a felony." Cool as ever, Victoria leaned against the doorframe. "We're not here to steal—"

"Detective," Shelby said, bravely inserting her body between Victoria and the cop, "we're here to pick up some papers for…a friend."

Even to her own ears, the excuse sounded lame, but Victoria's confidence—as well as her comfort in having her father's powerful law firm on speed dial—wasn't going to fly with this guy. He looked fully capable of breaking rules, bones and laws to get what he wanted.

Those piercing eyes shifted their attention to Shelby. "Uh-huh. When did you get to be such good buddies with Max Banfield?"

"Well…" Shelby swallowed. "I catered a party for him recently, and we started talking, and…"

Victoria, her stride lithe and self-assured, moved toward them. "Are you arresting us for something?"

"How 'bout I start with trespassing?" he returned. "Maybe add in a little burglary?"

Victoria smiled as she pulled out her cell phone, and Shelby's stomach bottomed out. Surely this was a bluff. She absolutely did not want to end this night with an encounter involving her friend's austere father.

"Do you always wear gloves to retrieve papers for a friend?" the detective asked.

"It's the latest high-fashion fad," Victoria said, flipping her covered hand so calmly Shelby nearly believed her.

Antonio bowed his head, then shook it, obviously frustrated with the alternating lobs of lame and aggressive answers.

Calla rounded the desk, stopping mere inches from the cop. He lifted his head, as if he sensed her closeness. "Have you been following me?"

"Yes," he admitted. "And with good reason. Do you realize how much trouble you'd be in if anybody else had found you here?"

Calla jerked up her chin. "We had to do something about this case. You're not."

"I am. Though I'm obviously not doing it fast enough to suit you. I knew you'd do something desperate."

"But you're not going to arrest us."

"I ought to," the detective said, though he was clearly torn. "A night in lockup would do you a world of good."

Calla brushed her lips across his cheek. "Thanks."

The detective's gaze met Calla's for one humming moment before she stepped back.

"So glad that's settled," Victoria said, her tone amused. She dropped her phone back into her jacket pocket. "How about we all go down to Cooper's Pub for drinks?"

Looking grateful for breaking the tension, Calla smiled. "Sounds fun. Detective, I don't think I've formally introduced you to my friends."

Antonio pointed at Victoria. "Victoria Holmes, vice president, Coleman PR. Daughter of Stuart and Joanne, NYC VIPs, attorney and surgeon respectively." Nodding at Shelby, he continued, "Shelby Dixon of Savannah, Georgia, transplant to the city. Owner Big Apple Catering, daughter of recently fleeced victims John and Nancy." He lifted his lips in what might have been a smile. "Leader of the gang."

"We're not a gang," Calla insisted.

Antonio looked skeptical. "Organized effort at B&E in the middle of the night, complete with lookout. Preplanned gear and manner to evade law enforcement—dark clothing, fleeting and guilty glances down the hall, subversive attitudes, you get the idea. Sounds like a gang to me."

Victoria scowled. "I'm not getting a tattoo."

"Of course you're not," Shelby said, squeezing her hand.

She'd started this. She'd led her friends down this road. She was the reason their backgrounds were being investigated.

The detective was right about everything. "We're trying to save my parents' future," she said to him. "I appreciate your concern and your thoroughness." She exchanged a glance with Calla, whose eyes were pleading. "As well as your understanding at finding us in this…unusual situation. But we're done waiting. Max is, even now, preparing to swindle again. We need to find out what, when and where."

"How do you know he's working on a new scheme?" the detective asked.

Since *we overheard him recruiting investors at a cocktail party* sounded ridiculous, even to her, Shelby settled on, "We just know."

Antonio stared at her in disbelief. "Yes, Judge Mackland," he said mockingly. "I'm asking for a warrant based on a local caterer's assertion that she *just knows* a fraud operation is being conducted in a midtown office building."

"We don't need a warrant," Shelby said.

Both realization and anger shot into his eyes. "Hell."

Calla laid her hand on his arm. "Have you talked to the witnesses whose statements I gave you last week?"

"Haven't had time," he said. "This East River homicide takes precedence."

"Not for us," Calla said, her tone gentle in spite of his obvious frustration. "You told me yourself that fraud is difficult to prove, that witnesses are reluctant to come forward. You haven't been able to stop him. We can."

"As long as you don't do it on my shift," he muttered.

He might not be prepared to arrest them, but he couldn't help them, either. Shelby knew this might be their only chance. She already felt lousy for involving Trevor in their investigation. She was pretty positive she'd feel worse if she didn't get this information herself instead of relying on him to get it from his brother—based on her lie, no less.

"Why don't you guys go on down to the pub?" Shelby suggested. "I'll be there in a minute." She looked at the detective, then away. "I want to straighten up, make sure we haven't disturbed anything." Her gaze—compulsively, it seemed—went back to Antonio. "You know, out of respect."

The detective didn't move, even when Calla and Victoria headed to the door. "How do you know?" he asked Shelby.

Shelby pressed her lips together. The less the detective knew, the better. For all of them. Yet she also knew he wouldn't relinquish control without a grain of confidence in her determination. Without some sense that they were, ultimately, moving toward the same goal.

She wondered if his conscience was as torn as hers. Did the end really justify the means? Retribution at any cost? Could justice truly be blind? Who, ultimately, drew the line between what was right and what was wrong?

"There's an investors' meeting," she said finally. "We need to know when and where."

He held her gaze, then jerked around and headed toward the door. "I'll be outside."

"I'M SURPRISED YOU HAVEN'T asked me about Max's investors' meeting," Trevor said to Shelby as he stood beside her in his kitchen.

"Oh." Shelby's gaze danced away from his and onto the beef filet she was rolling in pastry dough. "Did you find out something?"

Momentarily distracted by her hands molding the pastry and wanting her touch against his own skin, he endeavored to focus on the topic. "It's a long-term project. He's rehabbing an old artist space into condos and looking for tenants to buy."

Shelby nodded. "Sounds like a great idea."

"As long as everything comes together." The last thing Trevor wanted to do was encourage Shelby's friend into investing with Max. Maybe his brother would fit all the pieces together, but Trevor wasn't counting on it. "She might want to wait a few months before investing."

"She might, but Victoria doesn't tend to live in one place for long. And if it's a hot property, she could jump in." Washing her hands at the sink, Shelby glanced at him. "When's the presentation?"

"Next Thursday night at The Crown Jewel. Suite 1634."

"Okay. I'll tell her."

"You don't want to write it down?"

She used the towel tucked into her apron strings to dry her hands, then tapped the side of her forehead. "I've got it."

"You're in work mode and want me to leave you to do your job."

She leaned into him, laying her hand against his cheek. "I'm glad you're here…particularly since this is your apartment."

"But I could do something else."

"You could set up the bar."

He kissed her forehead, then moved into the living room to follow her suggestion. As he polished glasses and checked the stock of liquors, he felt a pang of regret for the upcoming party. Though the clients he was entertaining were important, he'd much rather spend the evening enjoying Shelby's exclusive company.

When everything was organized to his satisfaction, he reached into the back of the cabinet for a bottle of Johnnie Walker Blue. Ridiculously overpriced, of course, but then the best things usually were.

He poured a small measure into two glasses filled with ice, then strolled into the kitchen, where Shelby was chopping celery. "Do you drink Scotch whiskey?"

She wrinkled her nose. "Not really."

He handed her one of the cut-crystal tumblers. "See if this changes your mind."

"I don't usually drink with clients before an event."

"It's barely a sip. Besides, you could make an exception for me, couldn't you? I'm more than a client, after all."

Her gaze searched his. "I guess you are."

He tapped his glass against hers, and the crystal pinged. "To us."

She smiled. "And to perfectly done Beef Wellington."

"I have complete faith in your culinary talents."

As she sipped her Scotch whiskey, the warmth of pleasure lit her face. His body responded by hardening instantly.

Yes, he very much wished they could be alone tonight.

"Wow," she whispered, her tongue peeking out to stroke her bottom lip.

"I couldn't agree more." Though he wasn't referring to the drink.

His guests would be arriving in twenty minutes, and instead of letting his caterer do her job, he was plying her with Scotch whiskey and wondering how quickly he could get her out of her clothes. What was wrong with him? One minute he'd been relaxed, and the next he was fighting a tide of desire.

He took business seriously. He'd never have enjoyed so much success otherwise.

Maybe he was spending too much time around Max.

"Your place is beautiful," she said, glancing around, so hopefully she hadn't noticed the tension inside him.

He forced himself to follow her perusal.

Two walls of his corner apartment were windows, providing a spectacular view of the Manhattan skyline. The walls were gray. The floors wood. The furniture minimal, with clean lines dominating the design. Recessed lighting illuminated on artwork and showed off the spacious floor plan to its best advantage. The kitchen and living room were separated only by a long, curved bar.

The modern space of steel, glass and marble was a stark contrast to the ornate, antique-ladened decor that dominated his childhood memories.

Though sometimes he thought he'd ventured too far from home.

"Have you been here long?" she asked.

"About a year. It's a lot of apartment for one person, but I couldn't resist the view. There's a terrace on the roof. Would you like to go up?"

She glanced at her watch. "I can finish the salad while you and your clients are having cocktails."

Setting aside their glasses, he led her up the steel-and-glass block stairs to the terrace, which, unlike the apartment, burst with color. He didn't come here often enough, he reflected as he took in the many varieties of trees, climbing vines and flowers. A landscaping service took care of the plants, a cleaning service the rest.

"Ah, now this is more like you," Shelby said, running the tip of her finger over a purple pansy.

"How's that?"

"Warm."

He raised his eyebrows. "The apartment has three fireplaces if you're cold."

"I don't mean temperature. I mean more homey. You're a Brit. I figured you for a moss-dripping country house, old wood and busts cast in memory of some long-gone relative."

"That's my father's style. I prefer modern New York."

"Maybe so, but you could use one or two of these plants downstairs."

Laughing, he slid his arm around her waist. "The next time you come over, you can redecorate to your heart's content."

She looked at him askance. "Next time, huh?"

He captured her hand, sliding it up his chest to hook around his neck. "No clients to entertain, and I'll make you dinner."

Her eyes brightened with anticipation. "Okay."

Before he could stop himself, he'd covered her mouth with his. He deepened the kiss without delay, and she clung to him, pressing her delicate curves against his body to the point he had to stifle a moan.

Then she suddenly jerked back.

Her eyes wide, she blurted, "I need to check on dinner." She hurried to the stairs.

Closing his eyes, so he wouldn't have to watch her go,

Trevor fisted his hands at his sides and ordered his body to calm.

Shelby wasn't some fun and games girl he'd picked up at a party. She was the kind of woman a man had a relationship with, the kind you fell for.

She wasn't going to tumble casually into bed with him, and he found that the seriousness of taking that step didn't scare his bachelor soul as much as it had in the past.

But he needed to let her set the pace, and he needed to get his mind back on business.

At least for tonight.

8

LOADING THE LAST OF THE coffee cups into Trevor's dishwasher, Shelby pushed the door closed and leaned weakly against the marble counter.

She'd survived.

And she had no idea how.

She couldn't remember a more torturous night in her entire life. The food had been perfect, or so the guests had said. To her, everything was overwhelmed by the memory of the Scotch whiskey she'd tasted on Trevor's tongue. Every time she'd heard his laugh, or saw his smile, she'd had to grit her teeth to choke back a surge of desire.

She'd had to suffer through the sparkling female guests flirting shamelessly with him, while she rushed around the party in plain black and wearing an apron. The blonde wife of the company's CEO had been so obvious, Shelby had been surprised she hadn't offered herself up to Trevor as the main course.

He'd been charming and polite through it all, even sending Shelby a wink or two when the blonde said or did something particularly obvious.

He'd also helped her carry dishes to and from the table, brushing her arm, touching her hand. By the time they'd reached coffee and dessert, she was so jumpy, she'd nearly dropped an entire load of dinner plates on her way back to the kitchen.

From down the hall, she could hear his voice, speaking in that smooth accent as he said good-night to his guests. A shiver rocked her body. She had to get a hold of herself. She was here as the hired help, not a hostess. If she didn't locate her professionalism, and fast, she was never going to get another booking out of Trevor or anyone he might otherwise be tempted to recommend her to.

He appeared in the kitchen, tugging on his tie to loosen the knot and stealing every breath from her body. "That went well."

"Everyone seemed to enjoy themselves."

Stripping off his tie, he laid it on the counter as he unhooked the top button of his white dress shirt. "Do you ever have a drink with a client *after* an event?"

His proximity caused a trickle of sweat to roll down her back. "Ah…sometimes."

He trailed his finger down the bridge of her nose. "How about the rest of that Scotch whiskey?"

"Well, I…" If she didn't get out of there, she was going to offer herself as the appetizer, main course and dessert of every meal he might want for the next week.

"You have somewhere to go?" he asked, his intent gaze pining her in place.

Had his eyes always been that bottomless pool of blue? Was it a trick of the light, or was she losing all her senses?

She laughed, which, to even her ears, sounded desperate. Yet another sense going south. "No, of course not."

"You have an early booking tomorrow?"

She shook her head. "I have a wedding to cater tomorrow night, but most of the prep work is already done."

"Good."

Grasping her hands in his, he led them to the bar, where he pulled out a bottle from underneath the cabinet, then poured them each a measure into a crystal glass.

"You didn't offer this to your clients," she said.

"They get good. You get the best."

He tapped his glass against hers, and they each sipped, never breaking their stares at the other.

"Will you stay awhile?" he asked.

She nodded, not trusting herself to speak. The taste of the drink had her mind zipping back a few hours into the past, when he'd kissed her in his own private garden of Eden, when he'd held her against him as if he couldn't bear to let her go.

Again, he took her hand to guide her to the sofa, which sat directly in front of one of the huge living-room windows. Did he sense she was contemplating a way to bolt from the apartment, or did he simply like touching her?

Either way, she was grateful for something to hold on to.

After setting their tumblers on the glass coffee table, he reached around her waist, tugging the tie of her apron strings. "Do you mind?"

She swallowed hard. "No. I should have thought of it. I'll get hollandaise sauce on your furniture."

As she reached behind her neck to undo that knot, he stopped her. "Let me," he said gently.

When she was free, he folded the apron and laid it on the table. He handed her cocktail to her, and they sat side by side on the sofa, each sipping silently.

"I should have hired servers," he said finally.

As she'd been staring at his elegant hand, wrapped around the crystal tumbler, she had to jerk her attention to his face. He looked worried. "I appreciated your help, but I guess you could have spent more time with your clients if—"

"That's not what I mean." He covered his hand with hers,

sliding his thumb across the back. "I wish you hadn't had to work so hard."

Always the caretaker. But she'd been running her own business a long time. "I get paid to work hard."

"Aren't you exhausted?"

She was pretty sure she could sprint from here to Harlem, and she wouldn't knock out her nervous energy. Of course if Trevor wanted to volunteer another way…

She generally didn't sleep with guys after only a couple of dates. But then she usually didn't lie, connive and conspire, either.

"I'm fine," she said.

"If you're sure."

"I am."

Trevor drained the rest of his Scotch. Had they really run out of things to say? Maybe he was the one who was tired.

"Speaking of getting paid, I owe you a check."

He started to rise, but she selfishly didn't want to lose his touch. She held tight to his hand. "You're good for it."

"I'll get it to you before you leave."

Silence fell again.

"You're not often this quiet," she said, feeling stupid for needing to interrupt the silence.

"You, either." Sighing, he brought her hand to his lips. "I'm trying to resist the urge to seduce you."

Her throat closed so quickly, she found it hard to breathe. "Really? Why?"

"I have no—" He stopped, apparently realizing the question had nothing to do with curiosity. His gaze slid to hers. Whatever he saw alleviated his worry. "Thank God."

He yanked her onto his lap, and their lips met. He laid one hand on the back of her head, angling her face so he could deepen the kiss. She tasted Scotch whiskey and felt hunger. Her body pulsed with need.

It had been a long time since she'd given in to sexual impulse. And never had a man like Trevor answered the call.

She fumbled with the buttons on his shirt, and he solved the problem by ripping it open, then following up by doing the same to hers. She'd imagined he'd be more controlled at a time like this, but she found herself thrilled by his impatience.

The passion in his touch electrified her senses, the ones she'd thought faulty. They'd obviously been looking for the right stimulation to come alive.

She let her head fall back as he slid his mouth across her cheek and down her throat. With a flick of his fingers, he unhooked the front-clasp of her bra and filled his hands with her breasts.

She moaned and let the sensation overwhelm her. Briefly, she pressed her palms against the heated muscles covering his chest, then drifted downward, to the button on his pants.

Either determination or the promise of fulfillment made her fingers steady. She undid the button, then the zipper, her fingertips brushing the tip of his erection.

"Bedroom," he muttered, swinging her into his arms.

He set her down next to the bed, which had a steel frame and was covered in a charcoal-colored spread. "I need plants in here, too, I guess."

She gripped the edges of his shirt and pushed them down his arms. "Sure. Later."

They undressed each other with impatient tugs and a few rips. He swore he'd buy her a new shirt after tossing her tattered one onto the floor. Thankfully, he kept condoms in his bedside table, so the process of protection was a momentary interruption.

When he pressed her back to the mattress, his body braced over her, their gazes met and her heart stuttered to a halt.

She hadn't imagined the pool of emotion in his eyes. It was there so vividly, she felt the piercing need of it and the significance of the moment wrap themselves around her as surely as their bodies longed to join.

He kissed her as they became one, bringing unexpected tears to her eyes.

Then all she knew was pleasure.

They moved together as if they'd been born for the purpose. The frenzied hunger became long, deep strokes of discovery and wonder. His body was a combination of lean muscle and raw power.

She found a million places to kiss him, to slide her tongue over his smooth, hot skin. Everywhere he touched her in return, she caught fire. Every movement intensified her excitement.

As the scent of desire filled the air, the world around them fell away. All she knew was the rhythm of their bodies, the press and slide of his touch, their skin growing slick with sweat.

His muscles quivered from the effort of holding back. "Let go," she whispered, placing a kiss at the base of his throat. "I'm with you."

That was all the encouragement he needed. His hips moved faster, deeper, stronger. The coil of need inside Shelby tightened further. The tension couldn't possibly hold for long.

Even as the thought passed through her, her body pulsed, gripping him and bringing wave after wave of satisfaction crashing over her.

The sensations were so intense, she barely acknowledged him following her into paradise. She clutched him in ecstasy and gratitude.

He collapsed on his side next to her, his heavy breathing stirring the tangled hair against her neck.

Her head resting on his pillow, she turned her face toward him.

Damn, he was beautiful.

Even more so flushed and satisfied, his radiant blue eyes dazed.

She needed him more than was wise. Her life was a heavy, troubled mess, but she felt light in his arms. Maybe she was escaping, maybe she was running from her conscience, but he made her heart stop and everything else acutely breathtaking.

"You okay?" he asked, cupping her face, his thumb brushing her cheek.

She smiled. "Pretty great, actually."

He kissed her lingeringly. "Me, too." Turning onto his back, he held her next to him so that her head rested on his bare chest. "I was afraid I'd botch this."

She paused to stare at him. "Sex?"

He grinned. "No, I knew that would work out."

"Work out?" She thumped his chest. "Don't go all gooey and romantic on me."

He flung out his arm, then clasped his hand over his heart. *"For where thou art, there is the world itself. And where thou art not, desolation."*

"Okay, too gooey."

"It's Shakespeare."

She pressed her lips together. "Sorry. It's lovely."

"Dramatic, certainly." Clearly not offended, he tucked her head against his shoulder. "I was afraid to botch *us*."

As a picture of her and her friends breaking into Max's office flashed before her, she fought tensing up. "How would you do that?"

"We haven't known each other long. I didn't want you to feel pressured into sleeping with me."

"I haven't." How amazing was he, concerned about her emotional state? Especially since she was the one botching things. How was she ever going to explain this business with Max? "Though it's all happened a little fast."

He slid his hand down her back, both comforting and sending renewed tingles of desire through her body. "I know."

"Scary?"

"No." He kissed the top of her head. "Well, maybe."

"I think it's supposed to be uncomfortable…to a degree. There's something powerful between us, but it's fuzzy. Whether or not it'll come clear…" She shrugged. "Time will tell."

"Nicely put. Uncertainty is the reason I left home. I wanted some."

"You *wanted* uncertainty?"

"Yes, though I know it sounds strange. In London, my life was planned. It had been decided generations ago. I was supposed to follow the family legacy and go into politics, teaching or the clergy. I was supposed to marry a proper English girl of good breeding. And, of course, continue to breathe— just in case."

"Sounds cold."

He squeezed her. "I thought so, too."

"So you came to New York, started your own business and became a huge success."

"You make me sound bolder than I was. I did have a healthy trust fund to draw from."

"And a family who expects perfection."

"Yes." He turned on his side, so they faced each other. "What does your family expect of you?"

He was making himself vulnerable to her. He'd told her things, shared memories and worries she suspected he'd shared with few people. If she cared, which she did, she could hardly give him any less.

"They expect nothing," she said, meeting his gaze head-on. "They want my love, my respect. They want me to be happy. I want the same for them in return."

"Life isn't that simple."

"Isn't it?"

"No, but it should be."

He pressed his lips to hers, then gathered her closer. Their wrapped-around-each-other position had nothing to do with sex, but with understanding. Appreciation. Promise.

She immersed herself in his touch. Her revenge paled against her need to be with him, but her family responsibilities lingered, and she'd dragged her friends into this conspiracy, as well.

Closing her eyes, to both her obligations and her deception, she trailed her fingers across his chest. No matter how new their relationship, she couldn't continue to lie to him and sleep with him. She was going to have to tell him about the Robin Hood plot.

But when—and how?

Because she knew one thing for certain. Her parents did expect something from her.

They expected her to be honorable.

Project Robin Hood, Day 18
Continental Apartments, The Penthouse

I can't believe we're doing this.

Standing in front of his office windows, Trevor reflected on Shelby's statement earlier that day when they'd met at his apartment and nearly tore each other's clothes off in their haste to satisfy their need.

"I can't, either," he murmured to the empty room.

After spending most of the weekend in bed with her, he'd been unexpectedly called out of town on Monday and just returned to the city at lunchtime. In the cab from the airport, his fingers had tingled with the need to touch her, a weakness he couldn't seem to set aside. So he'd called her and asked her to meet him at his apartment.

Bold. Maybe even bordering on crazy.

But then his desire for Shelby was that powerful.

How had he survived four days without her touch? Without the sensation of her body becoming one with his?

She was right in thinking their relationship was moving fast. But he didn't want to slow the pace. He wanted more, more and more.

But was he being fair to either of them? His job was hectic, his family commitments complicated, bordering on impossible. Was he crazy to drag her into that chaos? Was this the right time to get involved with anyone, much less a woman he cared about as much as he did Shelby? Max was messing up his life for the eight hundredth time, and there seemed no end in sight.

In addition to the ridiculous and risky business decisions of the past—the hot-air balloons being followed by an Alaskan king-crab fishing business—Trevor now had to wonder where his brother had gotten the money to buy a luxury hotel.

Turned out their latest stepfather had not bankrolled him. When Trevor had called his mother and chided her for giving Max money, she'd claimed innocence. She'd actually laughed when Trevor had questioned her about the amount needed for the hotel purchase. Apparently the new husband was well-off, but not flush enough to hand over millions to a stepson he hadn't even met.

Max hadn't attended their New Year's Eve wedding, as he'd been mooching off a friend who owned a house on sunny Antigua.

So where had the cash come from? Building condos on spec was one thing, but a real-estate transaction would have required paperwork, legal signatures, a big, fat check.

Was it possible one of Max's long-shot investments had actually paid off?

Given his lousy luck at the card table and the debts he'd

run up from Vegas to Monte Carlo, Trevor didn't see how his brother had earned thirty million dollars gambling. Whenever he earned the slightest bit of a profit at a venture—the estate sale and auction house he'd started with a couple of mates from school came to mind—he turned around and blew it on a boat or car or monthlong ski trip.

So how'd he get the funds to buy The Crown Jewel?

Considering Max's attitude when Trevor had last questioned him, the only way he was going to get answers was to conduct his own discreet inquiries. He needed to stay informed, since not only would his father continue to question him, Trevor would certainly be expected to clean up the fallout and head off the media when whatever Max was up to went sour.

His office doorknob rattled, and Trevor didn't have to turn to know Florence had entered.

Her sigh was heavy. "If you're going to brood, you might as well go home. Or go find that lovely ginger-haired girl and take her to dinner."

His pulse thrummed at the image of Shelby. "She had to work."

"So take your lovely and loyal assistant to dinner."

Trevor glanced over his shoulder, not surprised to see Florence's bright pink lips pursed as she fluffed her highlighted blond hair. "Much as I'd like to I already have plans."

"Go out with a friend. Go to your fitness club. Read a book. Relax."

He shook his head. "I mentioned I already have plans, didn't I?"

"Humph. I bet with that ungrateful brother of yours. He doesn't count."

"I'll be sure to give him your best wishes when I see him."

"See him?" She charged toward the desk with the same determination she'd once used to convince him that without the ability to add and subtract, his trust fund wouldn't do him any good. "Popin, you need to stay as far away from him as possible."

Thirty years later, the endearment still made his ears hot. "I can handle him. Why don't you head home?"

She didn't move. "I think I should come with you, make sure he doesn't take advantage."

"He won't. I'm checking up, not handing over a check."

"I should hope not."

Trevor rounded the desk and kissed her temple. Though she wasn't officially family, she was the best part of home. "Don't worry. I have your idea about pushing out the baby bird under advisement."

Florence looked skeptical. "I suppose his lordship is worried about what the scoundrel is getting into and dragging you into the muck along with it."

"He relies on me to keep him updated," Trevor said neutrally.

"Just remember he needs you more than you need him."

Though Trevor nodded, he knew nothing was further from the truth. He wanted his father's trust and admiration. Maybe it was the curse of the second son. Maybe it was because he saw his father's struggle to be confident with his heir. Maybe he was a sap.

At the door, Florence glared at him over her shoulder. "You're not messing around on that ginger girl, are you, love?"

Trevor grinned. "A beautiful woman who makes cookies and doesn't care a whit for my bloodline? Certainly not."

As soon as his assistant left the room, however, Trevor returned to staring at the horizon. Brooding was apt. Florence wasn't one to mince words or feelings when she cared so deeply. She'd gone from being a caretaker, to a mentor, to a friend.

Though he'd had his share of women he'd *messed around,* playing at romance and true relationships, he wasn't playing now.

Yet the closer he and Shelby grew, the greater the chance she'd learn what a wash-up his brother was. Plenty of respectable women in London had tangled with Max and heard of his reputation to the point they wouldn't associate with any Banfield.

Not that anyone would say so publicly. The whispers and pitying stares his father received were almost worse. Frankly, Trevor wasn't sure how much more the old man could take.

Why he was more annoyed than ever by his brother's lack of appreciation for all he'd been given, he didn't know. Why Shelby was different, he wasn't sure. He only knew he did and she was.

And, he admitted, how deeply that passion would go might change the course of his life forever.

9

Hotelier Misfortune?
by Peeps Galloway, Gossipmonger
(And proud of it!)

Did you survive Tax Day, Manhattan?

My buns and my pocketbook (And you *know* that's a Louis Vuitton classic tote, don't you?) are still chapped. Not sure we're getting our money's worth down there in D.C., but that's a whole different kettle of fish....

Speaking of fish…a friend recently had dinner at Golden, the premier restaurant inside The Crown Jewel—you know the hotel recently bought by financial guru *(cough, cough)* Max Banfield—and his thirty-six-dollar entrée wasn't gently sauteed in butter and herbs as advertised, but fried beyond recognition.

And, no, darlings, I'm not transferring to the culinary review page, I point this out to draw attention to the real flambé, namely the chef shouting in both English and Italian that he'd had enough of the deplorable situation at Golden and he was "so freakin' outta here." (Not sure of the Italian translation, but it involved quite a few hand gestures, you get the idea.)

My friend overheard all this with several other diners, by the way, because Golden's recent transfer of ownership has also included cramming so many tables onto the restaurant floor that the waitstaff has to turn sideways, which is practically illegal in nearly every southern state.

Questionable management *and* a renowned chef on the run? Sounds like Golden—and The Crown Jewel, in turn—could be in serious trouble.

Maybe you should have your fish fried over in Brooklyn for half the price, instead?

Keep your ears tuned and your gums flapping!

—*Peeps*

SWIPING HER FINGERS THROUGH the long, platinum blond wig, Shelby stared at her reflection in complete dissatisfaction.

The hairpiece had come from a nearby costume store on 21st, but since they leaned toward the elaborate, she looked like a cross between Marilyn Monroe and an aging Playboy bunny.

With way less than C boobs and lacking a professional hairdresser.

This is never going to work.

She wanted her parents' retirement money back. She wanted Max punished. She was crazy about Trevor.

No way all those things could come together successfully. A soufflé destined to fall, a steak predetermined to burn.

At least the suit looked nice on her. Since it was Victoria's, it probably cost more than Shelby made in a month. Which led her to consider yet another negative in her life—the potential loss of her business.

No matter that she was trying like hell to make everything work out, everything seemed destined to clash. Her irritation was running over into her deception to her lover and her intense feelings for him.

She'd left him earlier as he'd tucked her into a cab in front of his apartment building. Supposedly, she was meant to be on her way to her catering space. Which she had gone to. *Briefly*. Instead it was time for Robin Hood to kick into action.

She pointed at herself in the mirror. "*You* are a bad, bad girl."

Grabbing her bag, she left her apartment and hailed a cab. Today, maybe today, this whole nightmare would be over. In her disguise, she planned to lure Max into letting him swindle her. Then the police would stop following her around and concentrate on the real problem.

Though Detective Antonio had been remarkably understanding about ignoring their burglary attempt, he was stuck "being Homicide's bitch," as he'd so succinctly described the night they'd all gone to the pub, so Max was living high and preparing to ruin more lives.

And that just burned her cornflakes.

Plus, if the cops ever did get close, the rat would no doubt sense the trap and simply move on to the next city or country.

And just how did her sophisticated lover fit into all this?

She knew Trevor couldn't be part of Max's schemes, but there was no way a man with his intelligence was completely ignorant of them. Maybe she was lying to him, but he wasn't telling her everything, either.

"An excellent basis for a loving and lasting relationship."

"Talking aloud to yourself is a sign of delusion," the cabbie informed her. "I'm right here, ya know. Like talking to a shrink."

"Are you married?"

"Was. Three times in fact."

Yikes. "I'm going back to talking to myself now."

He shrugged. "Suit yourself."

Shrinks and delusion aside, he got her to The Crown Jewel in record time. Let the subterfuge begin...

After paying the cabbie, she walked into the hotel, trying to emulate Victoria's confident stride and I-could-own-the-world-if-I-wanted attitude. As she crossed to the elevator, she felt a moment of panic when she regretted not asking Victoria and Calla to come with her.

She'd insisted they stay away, afraid Max would recognize the three of them together, regardless of disguises. They'd supported her so much, but she had to take this step alone.

Approaching suite 1634, she rolled her shoulders. She was going to ruin this lying, smiling crook and get her life back.

"THAT'S *fascinating,*" Shelby said, laying her hand on Max's arm as she smiled at him.

Max shrugged without modesty. "Yes, I do have a knack..."

From his other side, a dark-haired woman linked her arm with Max's. "Certainly you do, darling. Over there are some investors you should talk to." She sent an icy glare toward Shelby. "You'll excuse us, won't you?"

Shelby clenched the stem of the wineglass she'd barely taken a sip from. "Sure."

Knowing her plan's foundation was shaking, she glanced around the room, wincing as her gaze passed over the scrimpy crowd and the hors d'oeuvres table. She'd have been more effective catering this disaster. This wasn't a gathering of people flush with cash who could afford refurbished condos in the East Village. She knew that because everybody here seemed like she usually did, and she had no money.

These people were here to be seen, schmooze the future Earl of Banfield, have a free glass of wine, a complimentary plate of crappy food, then hopefully meet people flush with cash.

Max soaked in the expectant atmosphere like a fish moving

water through his gills. He showed off schematics of condos with spectacular views via a 3-D slideshow presentation displayed on the wall behind the food table. He assured everyone the project was "well under way" and the address would be "the" place to call home in six months.

As a completely biased observer, Shelby noted he promised neither too much nor too little. He was a pro.

At least her parents hadn't been swindled by an amateur.

Though, hang on—

The brunette who'd absconded with Max had guided him to a woman of about fifty. She had professionally coiffed silver hair—certainly not a costume wig—wore a gray suit and matching shoes that Shelby had seen online going for a price with a comma in it.

She looked capable of investing in something besides time in front of the mirror. So among the posers, Max had attracted some actual possibilities.

Hang on to your pocketbook, lady.

Clearly Shelby's was safe. Max had paid scant attention to her, much less asked her to stroke out a deposit check. What was she doing? A caterer launching her own sting operation? She felt like a fool.

Time to call for reinforcements.

She withdrew to a quiet corner of the room and dialed Victoria's number from her cell. "This isn't working," she whispered into the phone. "He's barely spoken to me."

"In that suit?" Victoria asked in disbelief. "The man's blind, as well as idiotic."

"The tacky wig is spoiling my look," Shelby said.

"I told you to dye your hair," Calla said calmly, obviously listening in on Victoria's end.

"I'm not—" Shelby stopped. She was lying to her lover and dragging her friends into criminal conspiracy, but she drew the line at *dyeing her hair?* Something wasn't working, all right. And it was her own sense of logic.

Her mania for justice.

Then, from the other side of the room, an unanticipated event changed everything.

Trevor walked in.

Her stomach clenched, and she must have made some noise out loud, since Victoria asked, "What's wrong?"

"Robin Hood's arrow just went way left of the target."

"What the—"

"Gotta go. I'll call you guys back."

Her heart pounding, she frantically judged the distance between herself, Trevor and the door. Max hadn't recognized her, but he'd only seen her once, and then in the capacity of a servant. He probably wouldn't have remembered her even without the disguise. But Trevor knew her well.

Every intimate inch of her.

Thankfully, the posers descended on Trevor quicker than they had the bartender. Women flirted; men jockeyed for position to shake his hand. He was definitely somebody with cachet. After so many years in the catering business, it was cheering to realize she could predict human behavior more accurately than some psychologists.

Her triumph was short-lived, however, as Trevor glanced slowly around.

Sipping her wine—for real, this time—she kept her face in profile and hoped the wig hid some portion of her face. At least Max was in the back of the room. As soon as Trevor moved in that direction, she was going to skedaddle, as her grandmother used to say.

When he took a few steps in his brother's direction, she inched the other way. A woman and two guys obviously weren't going to let Trevor escape them, so they matched him step for step, the woman keeping up a rapid pace of conversation that would hopefully be either fascinating or distracting enough to hold Trevor's attention.

Then suddenly, inexplicably, he stopped. His head snapped in her direction. She sucked in a quick breath, and for a heartbeat, they stared at each other.

He blinked first, and she nearly broke into a run as he spoke to the people around him just before he strode toward her.

Her heart pounded as if she were an animal trapped in a cage.

Tough it out, girl. Maybe he didn't recognize her at all. Maybe he simply liked her suit. Maybe he wanted to know where she'd bought her wig.

"Shelby, what are you doing here?" he asked when he reached her side.

"Well, hell."

"That wig is awful," he said, his tone amused but his eyes conveying his confusion at seeing her. All the pieces hadn't fallen into place yet—her asking about the meeting for Victoria's sake, who was nowhere in sight, her telling him they couldn't go out tonight because she had a catering job.

She licked her bottom lip. "I can explain."

He slid his hands into the pockets of his suit pants and waited.

"Meet me in the lobby in ten minutes," she blurted.

Then, she skedaddled.

SITTING NEXT TO SHELBY at the lobby bar, a glass of fine Scotch in his hand, Trevor fought for calm. "You don't have a catering job tonight, do you?"

She played with the stem of her wineglass and didn't look at him. "No."

"You lied to me."

"Yes."

He clenched his hands around his glass and resisted the urge to hurl it into the mirror behind the bar. "Would you mind telling me why you said you do?"

"I'm sorry," she said, looking at him finally.

He noted the bleak expression in her eyes and fought to remain calm. "For what?"

"For lying. For what I have to tell you."

In the time she'd fled Max's investors' meeting, she'd taken off the ridiculous wig, false eyelashes and heavy makeup. She was Shelby again. Although she was Shelby before, too, even with the additions. She couldn't hide the way she stood and held her body, her lovely face, those inviting lips. Not from him.

"Okay." He couldn't think of anything else to say.

"Your brother swindled my parents out of their retirement savings."

"He—" Trevor shook his head, hoping to clear it. Whatever he'd been anticipating, that hadn't been it. "Max? The guy upstairs?"

"Yes."

He let out a laugh, then sipped his drink. "You're mistaken."

"I'm not."

She proceeded to tell him about the fraudulent investment schemes, Max cashing checks from seniors, then skipping town. Cops were investigating, though so far they didn't seem prepared to make an arrest. And Shelby and her friends had decided to take matters into their own hands when the wheels of justice weren't rolling along rapidly enough to suit them.

Project Robin Hood.

And what a fairy tale it was.

"Max is irresponsible, but he's harmless," he told her firmly.

Her eyes widened. "Do you consider swindling retirement money out of seniors harmless?"

"Absolutely n—" He stopped. This whole thing was a mistake. It had to be. "He wouldn't do that. I'll admit he frequently makes poor decisions, gambles too much and his grand ideas don't usually work out, but he wouldn't deliberately con anyone."

"But he has."

"He hasn't."

"I have proof."

"Where?"

"Not with me. It's at my apartment. The cops have a copy, too. Your brother won't get away with another scheme. I'm going to make sure of it."

"Well, I certainly hope your future efforts are better than this evening's debacle. Cheap disguises aren't your forte, my dear."

"It was going just fine until you showed up."

"So it's *my* fault you had to abandon your undercover operation? Didn't cast me in a role for your little drama? You slept with me to spy on me, I guess. To see if I was part of Max's latest scheme."

She looked away quickly, and his heart jumped.

He'd made the wild accusation because she'd hurt him by lying, and because he didn't want to face his own doubts about Max, didn't want to believe he'd sunk so low.

But it was true. He could see it in her eyes. He was a pawn in her plot for revenge.

He set aside the rest of his whiskey because he wanted its burn down his throat just a little too much. His body went numb all on its own.

She laid her hand over his, and the pain, somehow, expanded in a radiating wave. "I slept with you because I like you. I like you a great deal." Determined, she searched his gaze until he held hers. "But I did accept your first dinner invitation hoping to find out more about Max. I wanted to be sure you weren't part of his fraud."

"And since I passed, you decided to climb into my bed willingly." He snatched his hand away. "Thanks."

"Trevor, please. I know I made a mistake by lying to you. But the only thing I wasn't completely honest about was Max. Everything between us has been real and…wonderful."

"It *was*."

"You don't want to see me anymore?"

How could he? He'd turned to ice. "No, I don't."

"Okay." She reached into her bag and pulled out a ten-dollar bill, which she set on the bar as she rose. "Please don't invest with Max. I'm sorry, but he really is a swindler, and I'm going to see that he pays."

Trevor said nothing.

The fact that she'd accused his brother of unsubstantiated fraud was minor compared to his relationship with her crumbling like ancient stone.

He hadn't been made a fool of in romance since sometime in primary school. Yet his need for Shelby had blinded him to her true motives, to the harsh truth that she'd been using him to get to his brother. He was a dupe. Nothing more.

If he could only convince himself of that fact, he'd be free.

Project Robin Hood, Day 19, 4:00 p.m.
Javalicious Cafe, Midtown Manhattan

"HERE ARE THE PICTURES Shelby took at the investors' meeting." Calla slid a disk across the table to Detective Antonio. "They're not too great. She took them with her cell phone."

"While trying to be covert."

Calla nodded. The coffee she usually enjoyed had left a

bitter taste in her mouth. "Um, the covert part didn't go so well."

"I really am working on the case," the detective assured her. "She didn't have to screw up her love life."

Calla worked up a smile. "Sympathy, Detective? How unlike you. I should get you out of the office more often."

His gaze held hers for a fraction longer than was professional, the fathomless green seeming to draw her closer. "I can be pleasant."

"So I see. We've been sitting here for nearly fifteen minutes and you have yet to warn me off your case."

He scowled. "That's about to change. You and your friends need to back off. Banfield obviously didn't buy her as a potential investor, and his jilted brother is bound to tell him about the three of you trying to spoil his plans. Leave this to the professionals."

Calla shook her head. "No can do. Shelby is more determined than ever. She seems to think if she exposes Max, Trevor will forgive her."

Antonio shook his head. "Doesn't work that way in my neighborhood."

"I'm sure it doesn't, but people who cook well are often quite obsessive."

"So tell her to obsess over fruits from Bora Bora or something."

"Her mind's not really on delicacies at the moment. From what I gather, she's butchered quite a lot of meat in the last twenty-four hours. Did you read my story on Bora Bora?"

"I did. It sounded like a nice place."

"A nice place?" Calla rolled her eyes. "It's one of the most breathtaking, exotic, peaceful, romantic islands in the world. From the peaks of the volcano piercing the sky, to the water reflecting impossible shades of turquoise and emerald, it's almost impossible to capture its magic, even in pictures and videos."

"Right, nice."

She sighed. "How about you stick to your job, and I'll do mine?"

He tapped his finger on the disk. "Exactly my point. You and your friends pack up your disguises and save them till Halloween."

"Where's the adventure in that?"

"You appear to find plenty of adventure without sticking your nose into a cop shop."

Pleased, not discouraged, she smiled. "You read more than one article."

"I had to make sure you were who you said you were."

"You could have done that in a ten-second Google search."

Despite her pleasure, or maybe because of it, his stare was confrontational. "I like to be thorough."

"Me, too. Why were you suspended three years ago?"

Pain, then shock flittered across his handsome face for a split second before he blanked his expression. He leaned back in the booth and stared at his coffee mug. "I wasn't thorough."

Regret pulsed through Calla. She'd expected him to say in-house politics or the like. She certainly hadn't meant to cause him pain. She started to grasp his hand, but was afraid of making things worse. Instead, she linked her fingers in front of her on the table, keeping a safe distance from him. "Did you like my articles?"

"I read more than one, didn't I?"

Just when she thought they might become friends—or more—he withdrew again. *Calla, you really screwed that up, didn't you?*

As expected, he scooted out of the booth. "I gotta get back," he said, tossing a few bills on the table. "Coffee's on me."

"Detective," she called when he would have turned away. She held up the disk. "Don't you want this?"

He plucked it from her fingers, taking care not to touch her. "I'll see if our techs can clean up some of the images."

"Take note of the attractive brunette at Max's side. She could be an accomplice. She introduced herself to Shelby simply as Alice."

"Not Marion?" When she cocked her head in confusion, he added, "You and your buddies seem to think of yourselves as Robin Hood's gang. Wasn't there a maid Marion?"

"Marion was on our side." She pursed her lips as the casting slid into place. "And, actually, Trevor would be Marion for our purposes. Betraying the wealthy, unscrupulous side to fight with the rebels for truth, justice—"

He held up his hand. "Sorry I brought it up."

"You're right, of course. He hasn't exactly joined our side, has he? Well, Shelby is holding out hope."

"Right, hope." He shook his head, as if the concept was foreign to him. "Peaceful relationships aren't exactly my specialty, so tell your friend I'm sorry."

Watching him walk away, Calla sipped her coffee. There was a heart beneath all that turmoil, but its beat was kind of erratic.

10

Project Robin Hood, Day 19, 9:30 pm
Times Square

LONELY AND UNWILLING TO go with Victoria and Calla out to
the clubs for Friday-night fun, Shelby got out of the cab so she
could wander up the pedestrian-only portion of Broadway.

The bright-light craziness contrasted sharply with the inti-
macy of her neighborhood. The people she saw every day and
knew by name diverged from the dazed and dazzled expression of the tourists clogging the streets. The sights she took
for granted were glaringly present now—towers of steel, brick
and glass, cracked sidewalks, attitudes worn like designer
clothes. And noise, noise, noise.

Traffic was a bitch. Rent was beyond the reach of nearly
all. Dreams were made and destroyed daily, probably even
hourly.

Yet it was hers. Loved, feared and respected.

She'd come to the city to make it big, like millions of
others. And she was doing pretty damn good. No matter how
much Trevor meant to her and how much she regretted the
way she'd handled things with him, she wasn't giving up on

her dream. To do that, she had to make sure her parents got their own dream back.

He had to protect his family. She could hardly expect him to believe her, stand with her, when her goal was his brother's punishment.

So, for now, they had to be on opposite sides.

The evidence she'd promised him was in her bag. She wanted him to see it, but didn't want to bear the brunt of the anger in his eyes. Eyes that had once looked into hers with desire and adoration.

Regardless of his family obligations, he had a right to know who he was defending.

She walked over to eighth, which was considerably quieter and hailed a cab to his apartment building. Standing on the sidewalk after being dropped off, she looked up at the rising column of glass and steel and was pretty sure its tip pierced her heart.

The ache in the center of her chest spread, and for a moment, tears filled her eyes.

Blinking them away, she nodded to the doorman on duty. Thankfully, she didn't recognize him, nor he her. She wasn't sure she was up to explaining she wasn't coming to see her lover, but to further incite her enemy.

She walked to the security desk.

"Ms. Dixon, how are you this evening?" Fred asked.

She'd met him the night she'd come to cater Trevor's party. Had that been only a week ago? "Great," she lied. "I just stopped by to drop this off for Mr. Banfield." She handed him the packet of evidence she'd compiled against Max.

Probably confused, but too much of a pro to show it, he took the envelope. "Yes, of course."

"Thanks. Have a good night."

"You, too."

She turned to leave, then stopped. He was so close, and

she'd apparently lost all common sense in the last twenty seconds.

"Is he in, by any chance?" she asked Fred.

The guard checked his computer screen. "He is. Would you like me to call up?"

"No." She shook her head for emphasis. "No, I really... Could you please?"

Fred smiled and picked up the phone on his desk. He was probably familiar with babbling females asking about Trevor.

Shelby wandered a few feet away. If she overheard Trevor shouting to Fred *hell, no, that woman isn't ever allowed in my apartment again as long as she lives,* she was certainly going to lose it. As she paced, she crossed her arms over her stomach as if she could hold herself together with so little effort.

"Mr. Banfield would be pleased to see you."

Shelby ground to a halt and blinked. "He would?"

"Yes, miss. Would you like to take this up as you go? Or would you prefer me to deliver it later?"

"Ah..." She was still stuck on *pleased* to see her. Certainly Fred had added that part to be polite. "I'll take it." She clutched the packet in her shaking hand. "What the heck."

"You're cleared for elevator two."

"Thanks."

"Ms. Dixon?"

When she glanced over her shoulder, Fred was smiling. "He looked a little pale and distracted earlier. He'll be glad to see you."

Clearly Fred's detection skills weren't the sharpest.

"I'm sure he will," she said, proving her lying skills were honed to a razor's edge.

During the elevator ride up, she called herself crazy over and over. She nearly picked up the emergency phone to call Fred and ask him to cancel the express ride.

Drawing all the courage she could muster, remembering

she was a rebel at heart, she shuffled out of the elevator and down the hall. The apartment door was open. Her heart kicked against her ribs as if it was frantic for escape.

No doubt her instinct for self-protection.

As she reached the doorway, she realized he was listening to Sinatra. The icon's voice filled the apartment as if he might be singing into a microphone while standing on the dining-room table. "My Way" had never sounded so good or so desperate.

Holding the envelope against her chest, she ventured inside, tapping her knuckles on the door in a perfunctory announcement as she moved into the foyer and closed the door behind her.

No response.

Well, Old Blue Eyes kept singing, but no reaction from Trevor.

The effect was remarkably unnerving, probably his intention. He had a right to be angry, to blame her for ruining everything between them, to resent her for planning to get his brother arrested.

As she entered the living room, she searched the dimly lit area for him, finally spotting him standing in front of the windows, an amber-filled crystal glass in his hand, the city lights seeming to surround him.

"I was trying to get drunk," he said quietly, not turning around.

He could have punched her and caused less misery.

"I see," she managed to say. The tears sprung to her eyes yet again as she let her gaze rove his solitary form. "I'll set this down and go."

She was laying the folder on the coffee table when his voice startled her, louder and firmer. "Why did you come here?"

She could have brought the packet of information without

ever talking to him. She'd pushed herself to face him for one reason. "To apologize."

"You did that already."

"Not well." Commanding her feet to move, she crossed to him. Before he could stop her or she could change her mind, she laid her palm against his chest. She clutched his shirt. "I'm so sorry I screwed this up. I'm crazy about you, and I'll never lie to you again. I was desperate to save my parents, and I lost perspective. I have no idea how we'll reconcile this thing with Max, but I want to try. Please don't let my mistake ruin us."

His face was in shadow but she could smell the whiskey, somehow enticing and familiar even though she'd driven him to this dark point and regretted doing so.

"I never get drunk," he said slowly, his beautiful voice a bit slurred.

Carefully, she took the glass from his hand. "So don't now. Forgive me, instead."

Reaching out, he cupped her cheek. "I made mistakes of my own."

The relief rose up, nearly choking her. "Oh, yeah? Tell me all about them."

His arms surged around her, and she dropped the glass on the wood floor, where it shattered. But though she jolted in shock, his grip never slackened.

He tightened it instead, picking her up and carrying her toward his bedroom.

As he removed her clothes, he kissed every inch of exposed skin. The tenderness clogged her throat with gratitude. He forgave her with every touch, stroke and sigh.

Sinatra's voice continued its melodious seduction, clear and sure, familiar and renewing. His words accompanied their need, the movement and rhythm of their bodies merging as one. With full knowledge of all that still stood between them, they climbed walls and broke through barriers.

The hunger she had only for him filled her, drove her to happiness and fulfillment, reminding her that what was intense and sudden could also be warm, meaningful. Making her admit her feelings for this man were both complicated and simple.

They lost themselves in the night, in a legendary voice and passion that flew to new heights. And yet promised even higher soaring into the clouds.

When she faded back to reality, he was there, holding her head against his shoulder, his breathing sure and strong.

"You warned me not to give Max money," he said, absently stroking the hair off her temple.

"You shouldn't."

"I *should* have known I wouldn't be rid of you right then."

Raising up on her elbow, she pinched him. "Rid of me, huh?"

"I had a stupid moment where I thought it would be easier."

The desire was back in his crystal-blue eyes, and she found herself wishing she could stare at it forever. "I've had a few of those lately. They're hard to shake."

"Not this time." He traced her cheek with his finger. "You protected me. Even though I didn't believe you about Max."

"Did you tell him about my plans?"

"No. Did you think I would?"

She shook her head. "But Calla's detective friend warned us you might."

"Detective Antonio's a cynic."

"No kidding, but I still—" She stared at him in surprise. "How do you know anything about him? All I told you was his name."

"I have my ways." He kissed her gently. "Come on, let's eat."

Glad the volatile subject of Max was set aside—at least for

the moment—she looked down at her bare body. "We're not really dressed for going out."

"We'll find something here. You didn't forget how to cook in your despair over losing me, did you?"

She snagged his shirt off the floor and shrugged into it. "Luckily for you, no. I butchered a lot of meat, though."

"Can I pause and say *yuck* without sounding too unmanly?"

"Sure." She grinned. "I think you've firmly proven your manhood tonight."

WITH SKILL AND INGENUITY she managed to put together an amazing pancetta carbonara, which Trevor devoured.

He'd been running on caffeine, nerves and fear since the night before. The relief at being able to enjoy a meal while looking across the dining-room table at Shelby was powerful.

He held out his hand, which she took. "Let's talk."

As he led her to the sofa, he could feel tension spike inside her. He wasn't crazy about jumping into the trouble with Max so quickly after their reconciliation, but he had to let her know where he stood, what he'd discovered. In return, he needed to see the evidence she'd gathered.

Maybe, just maybe, they'd find a way to resolve this impossible situation.

"You're not the only reason I was upset tonight," he began, holding both her hands in his. "I've been doing some research of my own."

"About Max."

"Yes. I talked to Antonio and assured him I wouldn't warn Max, as he thought I would. Then I called a friend who's a bit higher up the chain than our pessimistic detective."

"How high?" she asked, her tone rising.

"A rung or two up the ladder of command. Max is in a great deal of trouble."

Her shoulders slumped in relief. "You believe me."

"Yes." He leaned forward, pressing his lips to her forehead. "I was wrong not to before."

He'd been duped all right, but not by Shelby, by his own brother.

"We all want to see the best in those closest to us," she said.

"I was worried about Max embarrassing the family name, about worrying my father. I wasn't worried about him hurting anyone else."

The brown in her hazel eyes darkened. "I'm sorry."

"You didn't do anything but try to protect your own family. Exactly what I've been aiming to do. Though without success."

He thought of the earl, of the upcoming conversation he'd have to hold with him. The disappointment and frustration that would follow. Then he recalled the last time he'd dragged an irritated Max away from Vegas—after paying off his debts—without so much as a thank-you for bailing him out before he got in deeper. He remembered all the empty promises Max had made to everyone in the family, swearing he was going to settle down, or at least stop humiliating the Banfield name.

Trevor was sick of the excuses and promises, the mismanagement and disrespect. Based on his friend's information at the NYPD, Max's future could be even more perilous than his past.

Damn, how had everything gone downhill so quickly? How had Max moved from poor decisions to outright fraud? It would be unbelievable if Trevor wasn't there to see it himself. His brother frantically treading water, poised to slide farther under the surface.

He would stop the slide, all right. Trevor was going to see to it personally.

"Do you mind if I stand?" he asked Shelby. "I'm not leaving you, I simply need to…move."

"You haven't failed, Trevor," she said gently, watching him walk away.

"I have."

"You have no control over Max's decisions."

"I should."

"How?"

The simple question fired his temper, something he rarely let loose. "Because it's my responsibility."

"Why?"

"Because that's what I do!" He slid his hand through his hair and tugged, hoping to get a hold on his frustration. "I thought I was doing it well. My family *expects* me to do it well."

"Max is clever. He works a room by being unthreatening, by not pushing too hard, by appearing to know less than he does."

"But he is all those things in reality."

"Which is why the ploy is effective."

"I should have known," he said, clenching his fist. "I've been bailing him out often enough, I should have seen what was really going on."

"You've been bailing him out?"

He heard the astonishment in her voice and held up his hand. "Not in the way you think. A lot of gambling debts and bar tabs, sure. I've paid off the paparazzi not to publish embarrassing pictures, but mostly it's been ridiculous stuff. He wanted to start a company that would give tourists hot-air balloon rides through Manhattan."

"There's very little open space. How would—"

"Exactly. It was preposterous. Then there was the time he bought a pair of fishing boats, intending to catch Alaskan king crabs."

"Isn't that really dangerous?"

"He was going to hire people to do the actual work. At least until he saw the insurance he'd have to carry on the business."

"Which I'm assuming he didn't investigate until *after* he'd bought the boats."

"You know him well."

"I'm beginning to. So how did you bail him out?"

"I found someone who could renovate the boats, add better navigational equipment and the like, then resold them at a profit."

"And who invested in the upgrades?"

"I did."

"Who got the profits?"

"I split them with Max. I'm not a complete fool." Though right now, he certainly felt like one. "I was trying to teach him something. To show him that mistakes can be recovered from, that a wrong step can sometimes lead to a right one."

"If you're you."

"Not only me. Anyone with a kernel of sense—"

She lifted her eyebrows.

"Ah, yes, well… You have a point there."

"And what Max is doing now isn't a mistake, it's on purpose."

He sighed. "I know. Buying the hotel sent off glaring alarms for me, too. I had no idea where he got the money for that."

Shelby looked astonished. "Retirement and condo scams would be a safe bet."

Trevor's stomach twisted. "You're undoubtedly right. But at the time of his big grand opening party, I didn't know. That's why I was there the night we met."

"You said you were there to toast his success, as I recall. You hugged him."

"I was there to find out how he'd acquired the hotel and to

warn him to stay out of the gossip columns. I wanted him to know I was watching him."

"That's why you were so suspicious of me and my friends," she said, her eyes alight with understanding. "Why you didn't tell me your last name."

"I didn't give you my last name for the reason I told you then—finding out about my family tends to make people change." Despite the seriousness of their conversation, he recalled her flushed face and direct gaze meeting his across a tray of crab puffs. He'd fallen hard for her and her succulent food immediately. "I liked you exactly as you were and didn't want to spoil it. But, yes, I was suspicious of you. I like to keep tabs on Max's associates."

She glared at him. "So you can buy them off?"

With a wince, he nodded. "I'm sorry to say I have before. *It's time to push the baby bird from the nest,* Florence, my assistant, is fond of saying. My lack of willpower has led to disaster."

"It's admirable you tried to save him, but you do realize he's a lying, no-good, son-of-a—"

He snagged her hand and pulled her to her feet and into his arms. "Such passion from the Yank. And my mother is quite nice actually. She has extremely poor judgment in matters of the heart, however."

"Nice to know Max comes by his lousy qualities naturally. How much of your time, money and energy have been wasted keeping him from drowning?"

He kissed her forehead and let her comfort wash over him, even though she was kind of annoyed with him. "Too much."

"It's pretty weird to be called a Yankee."

"Mmm." He kissed her the tip of her nose. "I'll keep that in mind." He kissed her cheek, then kissed his way along her throat.

She planted her hand against his chest and pressed back.

"You go over there. I'm sitting down. I can't think with you touching me."

Capturing her hand, he held on by his fingertips, which was a decent metaphor for their relationship. "But later...?"

A smile flirted at the edges of her mouth. "We'll see how it goes, Your Lordship."

"I've always thought formal titles were products of generations passed, and certainly not anything due me." He playfully tugged her against him. "But I'm beginning to see why my father enjoys the perk."

He pressed his lips to hers, lingering longer than he should, but not as long as he wanted. Then he led her to the sofa and stepped back, as requested.

"I went to the hotel party to see how Max had gotten thirty million dollars, which I suspected had come from our new stepfather, but wasn't sure. I never dreamed he was actually conning anyone. I went to the investors' meeting because by that time I knew for sure Max was into something sleazy. He told me about the real-estate project, converting the deceased artist's space to condos. I also learned he's romantically involved with the artist's former lover."

"Yuck."

"Well said."

"He's getting desperate."

"I agree. The morality and legality of his projects and his judgment are falling at a rapid pace."

"Desperate. You're so cute when you're wordy."

The unexpected compliment stirred him. "Come over here and say that."

She shook her head. "You need to read that first." She nodded at the folder on the coffee table. "It ain't pretty."

Trevor would have rather prodded a live snake, but he knew Shelby was right. Could it be any worse than hearing her say she was involved in her own undercover sting operation in an effort to expose Max's alleged crimes? Could it be any worse than two respected NYPD officers telling him his brother really was under investigation?

He looked through the folder with a sickening heart. Several statements by would-be retirees, including Shelby's parents, documented giving Max their life savings to invest in certificates of deposit, only to have him skip town with their money and leave behind only broken dreams and fake certificates.

Yep, it was worse.

The woman he cared about, who'd shared his bed and brightened his life, was a victim of his own brother's greed and unscrupulous behavior.

Still carrying the folder, he wandered around the living room. The scent of garlic, cream and bacon lingered in the air. The indulgent aroma reminded him of the people who couldn't indulge, who wondered how they'd make the next rent payment, how they'd survive without their savings.

While his brother cashed checks and looked toward the day the family coffers would open to him completely. While Trevor sat in his high-rise fortress of privilege.

He sat next to her on the sofa, close enough to touch, but still apart. The whole bloody business was starting to sound Shakespearean.

"Do you want to hit me?" he asked her.

"No." She glanced at him askance. "Though I wouldn't mind taking a swing at good ole Max."

"The line will no doubt be forming around the block any minute."

"It's already formed."

"I suppose it has."

But would he join?

He couldn't stand with Max against Shelby, but could he really battle his own family? Should he allow his brother to take the full brunt of the consequences of his actions? Especially considering Trevor had enabled him along the way.

Certainly he had to do something.

"When I talked to the police, they told me that though they don't have jurisdiction over the scheme he conned your parents with in Savannah, there's a complaint from Mrs. Iris Rosenburg, who lives right here in the city." He tossed the folder onto the coffee table. "Quite a resume."

"He gets around." She laid her hand on his thigh, and he linked their fingers. "And the past is quickly catching up with him—one way or another. When Calla talked to Detective Antonio, he agreed to reinterview Mrs. Rosenburg for further information."

"But he says there's a body in the East River—"

"Not anymore, I guess. Still, the detective has problems of his own. Not to mention there's something about him."

When she didn't elaborate, Trevor prompted. "Something about him…?"

"I'm not sure. Except that he's sort of supporting us and sort of annoyed we're invading his space. Mostly annoyed, I think. Oh, and Calla is hot for him."

"How wonderful for them."

She didn't comment on his sarcasm. She knew as well as he about all the barriers that remained between them.

"Detective Antonio also made an effort at convincing me to talk you out of going any further with your personal vendetta."

"Like I said, mostly annoyed."

"Did you really break into Max's office?"

She lifted her chin. "I'll refrain from answering that question without my attorney present."

"You didn't think I'd tell you the truth about the meeting? You had to get proof?"

"I'd already asked you to check with Max when my buddies came up with the alleged break-in at the office."

"And you didn't want to wait for my answer before committing the alleged break-in?"

"That, and I didn't want you in the middle. I didn't want you right where you are—forced to divide your loyalties."

"The evidence against Max is piling up."

"Knowing and acting against him are two different things."

The fact that she understood the position he was in didn't make the decision any easier. "Yes, it is."

"I guess you agree with the detective? You think my friends and I should step back and let Max go until the police can catch up."

He met her gaze directly. Brother or not, Max had crossed way over the line between right and wrong. As sick inside as he was about the whole business, he couldn't let Shelby and the others go on alone. And while he wasn't at the point where he could hand over his only brother to the police, he knew Max had to be stopped. "No, I think we need to handle this ourselves. I want in on the Robin Hood project."

11

"I HAVE A FAVOR TO ASK first, though."

Shelby's ears were still ringing from Trevor's announcement and not entirely prepared to hear his request.

"I've been—"

"Are you sure about this?" she interrupted.

"I am. Max can't continue on this path. He's hurting people." He stroked her cheek with the tip of his finger. "Namely, you."

"So you're doing this for me?"

"Mostly. Is that a problem?"

Her heart squeezed in her chest. "I guess not." At least not until she completely fell for him. Their relationship had started with lies and vigilante justice. They had nothing in common, other than Max and their desire. How could anything lasting come of that?

"I've been concerned about Max's behavior for a while," Trevor continued. "Babysitting him used to be easy, even second nature." He shrugged. "I watch him to keep him from embarrassing the family and the title we've held for more than two hundred bloody years."

"Because your father asks you to."

"Now, yes. Publicly, he's cut Max off. He was practically humiliated into doing so by his peers, even though I think he's convinced he'll turn around one day and find a clone of himself staring at Max's image in the mirror."

"You never told me delusion ran in your family."

Trevor's smile was as weak as her attempt to joke. "They must, since, in the beginning, I was truly trying to help. We're brothers. I wanted to support him. But I've been resenting him lately and feeling guilty about it. Now, given that his actions have gone far beyond embarrassment, I feel foolish."

"And angry? It's okay to be angry."

"Believe me, I am." He squeezed her hand. "But I'd like you to do something for me before going forward with your plans."

"And that is…?"

"I want to give Max an opportunity to apologize and make restitution."

She leaped to her feet. "No. Absolutely not. We're way past apologies."

"And restitution," he reminded her calmly. "Obviously, your parents are struggling. Their financial situation has driven you outside the law. If I can get Max to pay…"

"It's not only about the money."

"What's it about, then? Revenge?"

"You're damn right it is!" She attempted to pace off her fury, only to find her temper snarling even louder. Freakin' rich people. If they didn't like how their life was going, they bought a new outcome. How many demanding, irrational, privileged jerks had she placated and served and…

Whose checks she'd cashed to live the life she wanted.

Stopping, she curled her hands into fists and tried to think rationally. Trevor wasn't Max. And being a jerk wasn't limited to those with money.

Facing her lover, she crossed her arms over her chest. "After all the suffering he's caused why does he get to write a check and make it all go away? No. I want him prosecuted."

"You want him punished."

"And what's wrong with that? Too uncivilized for you, Your Lordship?"

Slowly, he rose to his feet. His blue eyes had hardened like ice. He clearly didn't like her mocking his family title, especially since she'd used it often as an endearment. "You want people to take the law into their own hands? To ignore rules and procedures? To decide who's guilty among themselves and pass judgment and sentencing?"

"There are times when desperate measures are needed."

"And who decides that? *You?*"

She certainly didn't want the days of the Wild West again, but when the law turned its back on hardworking, if somewhat gullible people, somebody had to step up and make things right.

The law isn't turning its back. Lady Justice is simply moving too slowly.

What would it hurt to give Trevor this opportunity so they could fight for the same side? Max wouldn't dish out a dime to her parents or anybody else. She'd bet her new deluxe convection oven he'd laugh in Trevor's face when he made his reimbursement request.

"Fine," she announced. "But I have no control over any charges the police eventually manage to scrape together."

"Agreed."

"And Max will pay. Not you."

"I'd be glad to—"

She glared at him. "*Max* will pay."

"Your parents shouldn't continue to worry. Let me help."

"I'm helping them."

"A loan?"

"No." Drawing a deep breath, she fought against the humiliation of her lover knowing she'd failed to protect her family, particularly when he was so adept at sheltering his. "Thank you, but no. This is my fight."

"Mine now, too. My family has lived by a code of honor, loyalty and civility for generations. I can't let this go."

"Neither can I."

"So we agree."

Close enough to touch, yet she felt as though they'd traveled miles in opposite directions.

She didn't like the distance. There would be battles enough to contend with. It'd be nice to have him beside her.

She looped her arms around his waist, laying her head against his chest. His heart beat soundly against her cheek. "Even if Max agrees to restitution, you'd better hire him a darn good attorney."

Sighing, he held her against him. "I will. Still, he's hardly a criminal mastermind. Certainly not front-page news."

She pressed her lips to his jaw. "The gossip columns seem to love him."

"Don't they just?"

"Bet Daddy isn't happy about that."

"No, he definitely isn't." Trevor's mouth twitched with amusement. His eyes thawed. "Daddy?"

"It's a Southern thing. What do you call him?"

"Sir."

"Not *my lord* or *milord?* That kind of thing?"

"In public, I do. In private he relaxes the rules."

Shelby rolled her eyes. The guy sounded like a true stuffed shirt. How fortunate was she that his son—the insignificant second one—was so deliciously passionate.

She bumped her hips against his. "I think *milord* is sexy."

"Do you?" He slid his hands down her backside and held her against his body. "Instead of getting revenge on Max, we could knock him and my cousin off, and I'd have quite a few titles coming my way."

"Oh, yeah?" She glided her tongue across his bottom lip and reveled in the way he tensed. "Name them."

"There's the Earl of Westmore, of course."

She unfastened the buttons on his shirt. "That's your father's title, right? Even without Max in the picture, you'd only get that when he passes away."

"True, but—"

She slid her hands across his bare chest, clearly distracting him. His skin was warm, but she knew she could make it hot. "So now we're knocking off three people. Too complicated. What else?"

"My second cousin's the Viscount Carlton."

"That's pretty hot."

"Is it?"

"If you're into that kind of thing." She shoved his shirt down his arms, then dropped it on the floor. "What about you? Without us committing patricide or fratricide or…whatever killing a cousin might be."

"Very formally I'd be the Honorable Trevor Banfield, but I have no actual title."

She unbuttoned his pants. His erection pulsed against her hand. "What a shame. I'd like you so much more if you did."

He closed his eyes as she stroked him. "You lie."

"See what a good vigilante I am?"

She backed him to the sofa and let go of him long enough to strip off her clothes. Naked, she straddled him, rubbing herself against his hardness, enjoying the building of tension, the desire that slammed her body and soul.

He braced his hands on her hips, encouraging her to rock with him. "The best I've ever seen."

Protection was essential before their hunger climbed beyond the point they could think. Before they became one.

Still…for the moment, she liked the teasing.

"Titles are kind of boring," she said.

He cupped the back of her head and angled her face for his kiss. "I so agree," he said hungrily before he captured her mouth.

He tangled his tongue with hers. The potency of his warm, familiar sandalwood scent, and the obvious need to be with her, have her, left her trying desperately to catch her breath.

"I was thinking we'd play master and maid," she said against his lips.

"You sure you don't want to be the duchess?"

"Hell, no. Besides, I already have a French maid's costume."

"Do you?" He tongued his way down her throat. "Make it an English maid, and you've got a deal."

She halted her teased rubbing, planting her hands against his shoulders as she leaned back. "You want to be diplomatic *now?*"

"I have to be loyal to the motherland."

"Uh-huh." She climbed off his lap and rose. "I'll get my stuff together, go home and sew a tiny little British flag to my costume." Glancing over her shoulder, she wiggled her bare butt and pointed at him. "You wait right there till I get back."

She'd barely taken another step before she heard him charging after her.

"Have pity, milady," he rasped in her ear as he lifted her off her feet and carried her to his bed.

Project Robin Hood, Day 22
Office of Maxwell Banfield Inc.

"TELL ME ABOUT FIRST RATE Investments," Trevor asked his brother on Monday morning.

"It was a business I owned for a while. Things didn't work out."

Typical Max. Nothing concerned him except his own neck.

Was he oblivious even now to the grave jeopardy he was in? Did he have any instinct about how far apart they'd grown in the last few days?

Trevor glanced around the office. It communicated confidence and prosperity but seemed overdone. Trevor had always noticed something was wrong. Because Max had poor taste or because there was something truly wrong?

"Mind if I sit?" Trevor asked him casually.

Deliberately insulting, Max glanced at his watch. "I have a meeting in twenty minutes."

Trevor held on to his temper just barely. He thought of Shelby, of how much she meant to him. Of how desperately he wanted this whole disaster over with, so he could concentrate on her. On them.

In between her catering jobs, he and Shelby had spent the weekend in bed. Again.

He was starting to see a pattern form, and he liked the picture.

"This won't take long," Trevor said, lowering himself into the chair in front of Max's desk. He and Shelby had come up with a strategy, and he hoped to hell it worked. "One of your former clients came to me and said you swindled her and her husband out of their retirement savings."

Max's casual pose and expression disappeared. "Who? When?"

"It hardly matters. Did you?"

"Did I what?"

"Swindle them."

"Of course not." Max clenched his hands together. "How could you ask me something like that? I connect people with good deals, but not every investment works out."

"Invest in what?"

"For retirees I generally recommend CDs."

"CDs are pretty secure." *Unless there are no CDs.*

"Who are these people?"

"The Rosenburgs. Nice couple. Even nicer apartment on Park."

"I remember them," Max said, nodding sagely, though Trevor caught the whiff of another false note. His brother had no memory of taking their hard-earned money. "Shame the project didn't pan out."

"How did the…" Trevor bit back the word *scheme* "…project fall apart?"

Lurching to his feet, Max shrugged. "I don't really remember."

"Think."

Max's gaze darted to Trevor. His tone had burst his brother's self-indulgent bubble.

"You have to reimburse your clients."

"No, I don't. I told them there are risks with any investment."

"But you didn't invest the money."

"I gave it to a friend to invest."

The accusation had been a guess. One he was disheartened to have confirmed. "What friend?"

"A—a stockbroker." Max's face flushed—either from anger or embarrassment. Or guilt. "He's the one who said he was buying CDs. Get the money from him."

Trevor didn't believe him. Seeing his brother through Shelby's eyes had changed him. There was no friend. He'd never intended to invest the money.

And yet, whether it was old habits or protective instincts, Trevor couldn't resist giving Max one last opportunity to save himself. A window to crack and reap the benefits of having powerful family backing. "Your friend skipped town with the money. It's your responsibility to compensate the clients who trusted you with their savings."

"All my funds are tied up in other projects."

"Sell the hotel and get the money."

Max laughed. "You're not serious."

Trevor stood. "I am."

"I've done nothing wrong. Is there anything else? I have business to see to."

Trevor wished his conscience would clear. He'd given Max every benefit he could think of, only to have his offers rejected. Yet his brother couldn't possibly know the extent of forces moving against him.

For that, Trevor was sorry.

"You're making a mistake," he said quietly as he turned and left the office.

"EAT THIS. YOU'LL FEEL better."

Trevor stared at the huge cupcake with pink icing Shelby offered and shook his head. "I don't see how." But the damn thing was so silly—and it was Shelby offering it, after all, so he bit into the treat anyway. "You knew it wouldn't go well."

"It didn't go well?" Calla asked gently.

He'd come to Shelby's catering space as promised after the meeting with Max. He hadn't expected to find her friends Calla and Victoria there, too, but he should have. The whole gang was officially gathered together.

Even though he was wild for Shelby, he could see how any number of men would be distracted by her mates—serious, but glamorous Victoria and ethereal blonde Calla, whose name, as well as the frothy cupcake, suited her kind tone of voice.

"He laughed at me," he admitted to the ladies.

"Damn." Victoria reached for her purse. "Shel, I owe you twenty."

Seeing Trevor's confusion, Calla explained, "Victoria bet Shelby that Max would beg you to save him."

"And Shelby bet on laughter?" he asked.

"Yep." Calla shook her head, either at the entire mess or possibly at Shelby's inexplicable prognosticating skills. "I thought he'd go crying to Mama."

"You know him well," Trevor said, his gaze locking on Shelby's.

She rubbed his shoulder. "I'm sorry."

As he sat on the stool next to the kitchen's center island, he pulled her between his legs and wrapped his arms around her waist. He hadn't realized how much he needed her understanding until now. "He was a complete ass."

"I was afraid of that."

He tried to smile. "Not *I told you so?*"

"Not this time." She stroked his cheek. "You had to try."

He captured her hand, kissing her palm. He wanted to hold her, taste her, lose himself in her touch, but knew indulgence was a luxury. His needs would have to wait.

"How sweet," Victoria commented, clearly impatient.

Calla sighed. "Isn't it just?"

"I have a one o'clock meeting," Victoria said. "Could you guys make out later?"

Trevor aimed a genuine smile at Shelby. "Absolutely. What's our next step, Ms. Hood?"

"Cute." Shelby squeezed his hand before she stepped back and faced her friends. "We set a trap."

"That didn't work out so well at the investors' meeting," Calla said, her gaze darting to Trevor.

"So we plan better this time," Shelby said.

"A better disguise might be a good first step," Victoria pointed out.

"And we do it together," Calla insisted. "Last time you went alone. This time, we're together, whatever the plan."

"Maybe," Shelby hedged. "We'll have to see how things work out."

"We broke into—"

Shelby waved Victoria off before she could finish her sentence.

"I'm part of the gang now, right?" Trevor asked. "Don't I get to learn the secret handshake?"

Victoria poured more coffee into her mug, then refreshed everyone else's cups. "I was going to say we broke into Max's office together."

"And got caught," Shelby reminded her.

"There's a trend of us getting caught," Calla said, looking worried. "Maybe we should leave this to the police."

Victoria pursed her lips. "What a shame, especially since we were going to appoint you detective liaison."

"What's that—" Calla stopped and narrowed her eyes. "You're teasing me cause I have the hots for Devin."

"Do you?" Victoria asked, clearly delighted. "I had no—" She stopped her taunting after a sharp look from Shelby. "We can't stop now. We're finally getting somewhere."

"They're right, Shelby," Trevor said. "You started this together. You have to let them—and me—help."

"I will. I am," she added with more force. "But you also need to understand what you're risking. What if the unpredictable Detective Antonio decides to arrest us all for interference or whatever?"

"That would be obstruction of justice," Calla said, scowling. "Very difficult to prove, especially since we're helping justice."

Victoria sipped her coffee. "Bottom line? We need new evidence to bring to the police, something that will force them to step up their investigation."

"Where are we gonna get that?" Calla asked. "We've talked to everybody we can find that Max swindled."

"What about this new condo thing? That can't be legit." Victoria looked to Trevor for confirmation.

"Based on Max's recent track record, I'd say he's not being

completely honest with his investors." He paused. He had to shift his thinking. Instead of protecting him, he had to reflect on ways to prosecute his brother. It was a disturbing, if necessary, change. "At best he's using the new investors' money to fund the condos. There's no way he has the capital to start construction on his own. At worst, he has no intention of building anything."

Clearly frustrated, Shelby shook her head. "So we wait for him to cash the checks of new victims, wait some more to see whether or not he builds the condos, then drag everybody to the cops' front door?"

Calla lifted her finger. "Ah, sorry, but that doesn't sound like a well thought-out plan."

"Are we capable of coming up with a better plan over coffee and cupcakes?" Victoria asked.

Shelby frowned. "What's wrong with my cupcakes?"

"They're delicious," Calla said. "I think Victoria was wondering if we should have a more serious venue. And more time to consider all the options."

Shelby planted her hands on her hips. "You think we're gonna come up with a brilliant plan if we go to a boardroom?"

"Maybe it would help if we gathered in Sherwood Forest," Victoria returned.

"Ladies," Trevor began as he stood. Diving into the fray between three women was no doubt a homicidal endeavor, and he dearly wished he had the NYPD and their sharpshooters as backup, but with tempers and frustration running high, he was hoping to head off a major disagreement. "Between the four of us, our brilliant minds, research expertise, plus a bit of cunning and guile, I think we can find a way to fool Max."

"Oh, wow." Calla blinked. "He is good."

Victoria's icy eyes gleamed. "Are you sure you don't have a brother I can seduce?"

In addition to being into Shelby, he was utterly charmed

by her friends. Despite his family's track record with relationships, he felt oddly at home. "I do, in fact, have a brother. Unfortunately, he's the guy we're trying to send to prison."

Silence permeated the kitchen. Even the fan in the convection oven, cooking the next batch of cupcakes, seemed to stop rotating.

Then the ladies started laughing. Calla broke first, and the others followed. They hugged each other, and he stood apart, yet he felt privileged to be present at all.

Smiling, he leaned against the counter. "If anybody's interested…you might want to know Max is likely using swindled funds to keep the hotel running. Maybe there's an angle we can use there.

"I promise I'll help you. We're going to find a way to punish Max and get back the money." He approached them so he could link hands with Shelby. "You're not alone anymore."

12

"MY FRIENDS LIKE YOU," Shelby said, pressing her lips to Trevor's bare shoulder.

He dragged his mouth across her jaw. "I like them."

They lay side by side, replete from sex and still tangled together as if touching each other might be banned in the next hour.

The warmth of his body, the scent of his skin, enveloped her in desire and comfort. The conflicts and problems they were facing seemed a distant concern, even inconsequential.

She glided her hand across his chest, and his muscles twitched in response.

"I like you better, though," he said, slipping his arm around her to pull her against him.

She linked her arms around his neck as his mouth found hers. His tongue moved past her lips, and arousal flowed down her back, tingling all the way to her toes.

When they parted, she trailed kisses down his throat. "You like touching me."

He moved his hands down to cup her backside. "Every chance I get."

"I don't mean only now. Whenever we're together."

"You're very touchable."

"It's more than that."

His eyes looked starkly blue against the white sheets and his glossy black hair. "My father is restrained. I promised myself a long time ago I'd be different."

"Your father stamps out passion."

"He's not vindictive, just extremely proper. Are you trying to kill the mood?"

"I'm trying to find out things about you."

"Like what?"

"Anything. Everything. I can predict Max's moves easier than I can yours."

"I would hope I'm a bit more complex than him."

She smiled. "Good point. So your dad's restrained, which I'd pretty well guessed. What's your mom like?"

"Not restrained." He trailed his finger along Shelby's thigh. "She's like you—she says what she thinks."

"Does she? How did she get the attention of a restrained English earl?"

"By being blond and buxom. This is a very odd conversation to have naked."

"You want to get dressed?"

"No."

"So I guess you have your dad's coloring."

"Most of the Banfield men have dark hair, if that's what you mean. Max is the odd mix."

"In more ways than his appearance." She slid her fingers through Trevor's hair. Its silky texture sent a flare of need deep inside her belly. "Is your dad as good-looking as you?"

"He's an uppity Brit who bedded and married a wild, spontaneous, stunning buxom blonde. He's got some game."

"Do you guys get along?"

"As long as I do what he says."

Playfully, she poked his shoulder. "Come on. You can do better than that."

"We have a decent relationship, though we had some rough times when I was a teenager and resentful of Max the Would-Be Perfect Heir. Like every father and son, I expect. He'd rather I wasn't an expat, and we're not especially close, but I know he's proud of my success. And he's glad I don't gamble at his private London club, then fail to pay off my debts."

The whole deal still sounded cold to her, but not every family was as boisterous as the Southerners she grew up around. "What about you and Max? Do you get along?"

"Now I'm getting dressed."

Trevor rolled out of bed. Shelby only got a brief glimpse of his leanly muscled body before he stepped into his pants and fastened them. Tucking the sheet around her, she bent her elbow and propped her head on her hand.

She couldn't restrain a grin. They shouldn't make sense together, but they did. At least in the moment. Damned if he didn't make her crazy happy.

"You have to get dressed, too."

She scowled.

He extended his hand. "Come make dessert."

Reluctantly, she did as he asked, though wearing his rumpled white shirt still carrying his scent, changed her attitude.

In the kitchen, she found peaches, eggs, marsala wine and sugar, which she made into a simple Italian dessert.

Trevor licked the first bite off his spoon and moaned. "That's incredible."

She pressed her lips briefly to his before digging into her own cup. "It's called a zabaglione. Be sure you don't say that instead of my name the next time we're in the throes of passion."

"It's not quite that good." He linked their hands. "Let's go up to the terrace."

Once they'd ascended the stairs, Shelby noticed an addition

among the abundance of bushes, trees and flowers. "Where did that come from?"

"I bought it today," he said, leading her to the chaise longue. "Homey, don't you think?"

She smiled wryly. "I do. Just one?"

"Ah, that's the best part." He reclined in the chair, then guided her down to lay back between his stretched-out legs.

As they finished their desserts, his warmth surrounded her like the blossoms on the plants. The vibrant, chaotic city lay below, but that was beyond the balcony walls. Inside those walls, they were cocooned in their own private world.

"Which one should go downstairs?" he asked, setting their empty glasses aside and tucking his arms around her.

Remembering how she'd said he needed plants in the apartment, a different kind of coziness enveloped her. "A couple of the trees, plus some pansies. They'll get plenty of sun in front of the windows around the dining room."

"You've given this some thought."

"My mom's into gardening. I think the instincts are genetic. Do you not want to talk about Max?"

Against her stomach, his hands tensed. "We'll have to eventually, I guess."

"Would you rather separate your lover from your brother's adversary?"

"Yes, but I don't see how."

Since Shelby had tried, and failed, she could heartily agree.

"Besides," Trevor continued. "I'm a coconspirator."

"Because of me."

"No." Kissing the top of her head, he squeezed her. "Well, partly. I do want to help your parents, but I want to get restitution for everybody else Max swindled, as well. It's my duty to—"

"This isn't only about duty." She turned so she could see his face. Barely lit by the city's glow, he still took her breath away. Maybe all the more because this mess mattered so much to him. "You want to help because you're worried about everybody involved, not just my parents."

"Sure I am. What he's done to them is wrong."

"But here's where we're different. I'm doing this for my family. If it wasn't for them, I'd be off making pasta and sauces and letting the cops do their job. You're here because you see a wrong that should be righted."

"I'm here because my brother is causing all the problems."

She turned on her side, laying her head against his bare chest. "But not only problems for me."

"Not only," he agreed.

"You're very noble."

He chuckled.

"You think the earl would approve?"

"In theory. He'd be happy if my nobility kept his name out of the gossip columns, but since it's his heir who's due to be nicked by the cops, he's going to fight us with his last breath."

The full extent of what Trevor was risking suddenly became clear. Would he lose his father's respect as well as his brother? "He'd side with an unscrupulous swindler over you?"

"Max is the heir."

Such resignation. Yet Shelby couldn't imagine the man who sired Trevor would set aside the law and all his principles to protect a son who cheated people to cover his own mistakes. She wasn't exactly up on British law, but surely he could disinherit Max if he went to jail.

"I choose to hold out hope for the best." She traced her finger across his skin, though she had the feeling she and the earl wouldn't get along, should they ever meet. "You're hurt by Max's betrayal."

"Yes."

His pain, encapsulated in one word echoed through her. "You tried to help him."

"I thought I did. Now, I'm questioning everything. Maybe I should have let him fail years ago. Maybe I'm the reason he's come to this."

"You're not."

"If I'd stopped him sooner, he wouldn't have had the means to swindle your parents."

She'd sensed Trevor's guilt long before now, and she wanted that particular obstacle gone. She shifted to stare at him. "Max made his own choices."

"So you've said. But he's going to cheat at least one of those people we saw at the condo investors' meeting."

"We'll contact them. Get them to help us. Or we'll talk to employees at the hotel and see what they know."

"That's too many people who could tell Max we're asking questions. If we're going to contact potential investors, shouldn't we be warning them?"

With regret, Shelby shook her head. "This is where you and I are gonna part ways on justice. What we need is fresh evidence. Like Victoria said. Something to take to Detective Antonio and say *here's what happened last week.*"

"And sacrifice other families?"

"What else can we do?"

He stroked her cheek, then kissed her tenderly. "We can enjoy the terrace."

Max was set aside—a neat, but necessary solution.

For now.

Eventually, they'd have to resolve the matter before moving forward.

Trevor tightened his hold around her waist and pulled her on top of him. "You can also tell me how good-looking I am."

"Can I?"

He chuckled, then pressed his lips to the pulse point beneath her ear. "Please."

She understood he was asking for more than compliments. He needed a distraction. "I was sandbagging." She let her legs fall on either side of his thighs. "You're breathtakingly gorgeous."

"No kidding?"

"Uh-huh. And when you smile, I get all tingly."

"Remind me to smile a lot."

Since she wore only his shirt, and he wore only his pants, it took minimal effort to lift, unbutton, roll on protection and have them both sighing in pleasure.

As Shelby rocked against him, she closed her eyes, wanting to vividly experience every stroke, every gasp.

His breath was hot on her skin; the night air was cool on her back.

When his tongue flicked against her hardened nipple, she fought to find her breath.

But she didn't succeed.

He overwhelmed her—in a good way. He challenged and intrigued her. And she wanted him like no other.

At times, when their eyes met, she could hardly believe his was the face she saw.

She stewed, baked and grilled. She whipped and stirred. She served.

She didn't lose herself.

Except now. Except with him.

Bracing the heels of her hands against his shoulders, she rolled forward, then back with her hips. He surged deeper inside her and shoved down the shirt she was wearing.

As his lips caressed her breast, she let her head fall back. She wrapped her arms around his head and held him closer still.

Tucked against each other, nothing could come between them.

He moved but still held her, never separating, as he hooked her legs around his hips, then hovered over her for a moment before sinking his body between her thighs.

She gasped as she encountered the bracing impact of the chair beneath her, the intense pleasure of him filling her. She saw the green of the plants, the midnight sparkling sky and the intense blue of his eyes.

His hands cupped her breasts; his mouth devoured her skin. She felt his tongue against her throat. His teeth nipped her earlobe.

The fire and beauty of what they were doing washed over her as she hit her peak. She jolted. Her body pulsed in time with his. She felt his breath against her cheek.

She was falling in love with him.

His touch, his words and his heart.

Lying with him, she couldn't imagine anything separating them. But Max was there, in a way. And if she ruined Max, would that destroy everything else? No matter what Trevor felt now, how he wanted to make everything right, how much he desired her, she knew the possibility lurked.

Was she willing to risk Trevor for revenge?

"Good morning, Chambers," Trevor said into the phone. "Is my father available?"

"No, sir."

Though it was 6:00 a.m. New York time, it was eleven in London. Time enough for the earl to have had his breakfast, make calls, address correspondence, but not late enough for lunch.

I left a beautiful woman sleeping in my bed for this?

Trevor made an effort to keep the impatience out of his voice. "Thanks, Chambers. I'll call his cell."

"I'm sorry, sir. It's unlikely you'll be able to reach him. He's in flight."

"To where?"

"To New York," the house manager said calmly, not realizing the bombshell he'd dropped.

"He's coming here?" Trevor said woodenly.

"Yes, sir. I thought you were aware. He went to New York this morning. He should be there sometime this evening."

"How…interesting." Trevor's grip tightened on the receiver. "Thank you, Chambers."

"Good day, sir."

As Trevor disconnected, he heard shuffling behind him. He turned to see Shelby heading toward him. As seemed to be her wardrobe preference of late, she wore only his shirt, her fiery hair was mussed and she'd never looked more beautiful.

Lazily, she wrapped her arms around his waist and tucked her head beneath his chin. "If you ever have the urge to call me before the sun comes up, resist."

The tightness in his stomach over his father's impending visit eased. "The last thing this city needs is a cranky, sleep-deprived caterer."

"A little coffee will help—especially since sleeping with you doesn't lead to much rest—but I think I can manage breakfast."

"Don't you want to know who I was talking to?"

"Do you want me to know?"

He wanted to share everything with her. Though they'd only known each other a few weeks, she'd become an essential part of his life. If they could get through this ordeal with Max, maybe they'd have a chance. "How do you feel about having dinner with an earl?"

She jerked her head up. "You know another earl besides your father?"

"I do, actually. But my father's the one who will be coming to dinner. Expecting to surprise me."

In a purely feminine gesture, she tucked her tangled hair behind her ears. "When did you find that out?"

"Two minutes ago."

"Okay. Is he going to yell at you?"

He nearly laughed at the mental picture of His Lordship, Earl of Westmore, in a screaming match. "No."

"But he's pissed about something."

"Undoubtedly."

"Max?"

"That's a safe bet."

"So we probably shouldn't tell him about Project Robin Hood."

Her calm acceptance dispelled his nerves. If anyone was used to his father's cold temper, it was him. He'd protected and defended Max at the earl's direction, he could hardly be blamed for this awful business now. His conscience reminded him often enough of the missteps over the last few years.

"Probably not," Trevor agreed.

She let go of him and shuffled to the kitchen, where she stuck her head into the fridge. "How do you feel about eggs?"

"I know I can make them." He took the carton from her hand. "You don't have to wait on me."

She took the carton back. "I like feeding people. You, in particular. It's a compulsion."

Before he could so much as blink, she was cracking eggs and whipping them together in a bowl. "I thought your father was all about manners and social etiquette."

"He is. When it suits him."

"So showing up uninvited doesn't violate some highbrow rule?"

"Probably."

"When will he be here?"

"A few hours."

She poured the eggs into a pan on the stove. "Where do

you want to go? I may need to meet you there, depending on how my prep work goes today."

"I expect our conversation will be personal. How about if I pick something up, and we eat here?"

"Take-out food?" she asked in horror. "Are you trying to insult me?"

"My father pops into town without notice. I don't expect you to cook for him."

"But you want me to meet him?"

It was a bit early for a meet-the-parents date, he guessed. But everything about this relationship was different from all the others. Plus, he had to admit a certain curiosity for how his father and lover would take to each other. "I'm going to have to tell him about Max—all of the evidence against him. I'd like you to be with me when I do."

"I'll be there, and I'd like to cook. He'll be less cranky if he's full."

"What a dreamer you are." He scooped the eggs onto two plates, then handed her one, while he leaned next to the counter beside her. "Okay, then. But I'm buying all the ingredients, and you're not serving us."

"Deal." She devoured her eggs. "I could use a kitchen assistant."

"There are quite a few things I can accomplish in the kitchen." He polished off his breakfast. Taking her empty plate, he set it aside and moved between her legs, which she wrapped around him. "Should I demonstrate?"

She smiled. "Mmm. That would be nice." But when he moved in to kiss her, she planted her finger on his chest and held him back. "However, since now I have a dinner to prep as well as my regular work, romance is going to have to wait."

He trailed his fingertip across her cheek. "Anticipation can be good."

"After we get rid of Pops, I'm all yours."

He winced. "You're not really going to call him Pops, are you?"

"Nervous, maybe?" She scooted off the counter. "Can I borrow your shower?"

"Depends. Can I join you?"

"Multitasking. I like it." She snagged his hand as they strolled toward the bedroom. "What would Max do if he thought his shaky operation was collapsing?"

"What do you think he'd do?"

"He'd run."

"Yes, I think he would. We need to be careful about how we approach him and the people around him. I believe I made that point last night."

"We're watching him, but keeping a low profile. Which dirty, low-down operation is the most vulnerable?"

"You're so adorable." He pressed his lips to hers. "I think the hotel's in trouble, and the condo investment is obviously his next target, but—" He stopped, as something she'd said sank in. "You're watching him? How?"

"We trade off. Victoria and Calla have been bearing the load over the last few days while I've been…busy with you." She let go of him and moved quickly toward the bathroom door. "I really should get in the shower."

When he caught up to her, he wrapped his fingers around her wrist. "How are you watching him?"

"The usual way—by following him everywhere he goes."

_13_

"It's about time you got here," Victoria said as Shelby climbed into her friend's Mercedes. "Max is coming out any minute."

"Sorry. My prep work took longer than I thought. How do you know Max is coming out?"

"I gave one of the valets twenty bucks to text me when he was on his way."

"With the budget of this operation rising like a geyser, we're gonna have to squeeze that putz's wallet until he bleeds to recoup our losses."

"Here, here."

"As if things weren't complicated enough, Trevor's father is coming to New York."

Victoria stared at her in disbelief. "When?"

Shelby glanced at her watch. "Anytime now."

"He just decided to fly over an ocean to chat?"

"Apparently."

"The timing can't be a coincidence."

"No, I'm sure it isn't. I expect he's come to complain to Trevor about how he's handling Max. Or maybe his viscount cousin has landed himself in a scandal they expect Trevor to clean up. Or maybe he's decided to actually appreciate the non-criminal son he has."

"Wow. Who curdled your cream this morning?"

Shelby grinned. "Actually I had sex and eggs for breakfast."

"At the same time?"

"Consecutively." She poked her friend's leg. "You should try it, then you wouldn't be getting those scowl lines around your mouth."

Victoria flipped down the visor and stared into the mirror. "What—" She shifted her glare to Shelby. "That wasn't nice."

"Sorry, I'm a little punchy. I didn't get much sleep." She smiled broadly. "You know, more se—"

"Oh, look, there's Max."

Instinctively, Shelby slid down in her seat as she watched the hotel mogul-condo developer climb into a cab in front of The Crown Jewel.

Victoria slid out into traffic a couple of cars behind him, and Shelby made a note of the cab's tag number, so they could be sure they were following the right one.

The cab headed south, so he could be going to his office, the condo site or anywhere between 42nd Street and Lady Liberty.

At a stoplight, Victoria flipped down the mirror again.

"Cut it out," Shelby said. "You're freakin' perfect, as always."

She raised the mirror as the light turned green. "My spa consultant should send you half the tip I'll be giving her when I go in for a full treatment tomorrow."

"Yeah, sure." How somebody as stunning as Victoria could have doubts about her appearance, Shelby would never understand. "What should I wear tonight?"

"Something besides Trevor's sheets."

"That's really funny."

Victoria shrugged and turned left as Max did the same. "It's a reasonable warning, Miss Nympho."

"Jealous?"

"Insanely."

"Seriously. Do I wear jeans? My chef's jacket? Your black Chanel suit?"

"Yes, no, and dream on." Victoria glanced at her. "Relax. He may be an important man, but he's still just a man. Puts his pants on one leg at a time, et cetera."

"I'm not worried about the title thing. But he's Trevor's father. If he hates me, Trevor's going to dump me."

"No, he won't. Trevor's his own man. Cook the father something. You'll feel better."

"I am."

"Pasta?"

"I wish. The earl is apparently a fussy eater. Basic meat and potatoes kind of stuff." Shelby wrinkled her nose. Culinarily repressed people weren't her forte. "I considered making escargot or *cervelles au beurre* just to be bold, but in the end decided on roasted chicken and vegetables."

"*Cervelles au beurre?* Isn't that—"

"Cow brains in butter."

"I don't even want to know where you get those."

Amused, Shelby angled her head. "I've seen you tuck into a prime filet a time or two. What's the difference?"

"Brains are icky."

To hear her posh, sophisticated friend say *icky* was truly funny. Which was probably why her mood didn't take a nosedive as she realized Max was on his way to his downtown office.

Same old, same old. No clandestine meeting with a loan shark or shady accountant they could document and add to their file of bad deeds.

Victoria pulled to the curb, and they watched Max alight

from the cab in front of the tacky Campbell Building they'd broken into less than two weeks ago.

They were approaching the one-month anniversary of Project Robin Hood, and they were no closer to getting revenge on Max than when they started. She experienced a whole new respect for the difficulties of Detective Antonio's job.

How much longer could she expect her friends to give up their time, emotional support and money for the cause? And was her heart even in it anymore?

Given the space Trevor occupied in her emotions, she couldn't cause him pain. And while this whole mess was certainly Max's fault, the doubts about whether or not she could go through with her vindictive plot were growing.

"If you need to get back to your chicken, I'll wait," Victoria offered, leaning her seat back and pulling her cell phone from her purse.

Shelby laid her hand over her friend's. "No. Let's go."

Victoria's gaze probed hers. "He could leave here and meet with one of his potential investors. Didn't you say contacting one of them was our best option? Don't we need new evidence to take to the police?"

"Yes and yes. But right now we need to go get a drink somewhere."

"It's not five o'clock."

"It will be by the time we get to Marque's. Let's set this aside for tonight. Tell me what's going on with you."

Victoria shifted the purring luxury car into gear.

SHELBY RAN PAST TREVOR as he opened his apartment door for her. "Sorry I'm late. I tried to do way too much, then I got caught up with Victoria's concern for her promotion, which she completely deserves, but—"

"Hey." He snagged her by the shoulders and pulled her

against him. His blue eyes radiated desire. "I missed you today."

Her heart fluttered.

He was freshly showered, dressed in jeans and a black sweater and smelled like manly heaven.

Victoria had been right to keep her outfit casual. She wore roughly the same thing, though she'd tossed on her chef's jacket to keep from spilling anything on her clothes while she cooked.

He captured her mouth, angling his head to give her a thorough welcome that drove away all thoughts of family, food and frankly anything but the flow of need through her veins.

Unfortunately, when they separated, reality returned.

She cast a glance down the hall. "Is your father here?"

"No." He wrapped his arm around her waist and led her into the living room. "He checked into his hotel a few hours ago, called me to say he was in the city, then informed me he was having tea, contacting a few people, and he'd be arriving at seven."

"Did he say why he was here?"

"No, but we know my brother is on his agenda."

"Yeah." She flopped her head against his shoulder. "I've had a martini. I think I'm loopy."

"Remind me to take advantage of you later."

"That sounds—" She halted as they reached the end of the hall. "Oh, my." Trees, bushes and flowers suffused the living and dining rooms. Not the jungle of the terrace, but an artful setting that fit Trevor exactly. "You've been working hard today."

Embracing her from behind, he placed a lingering kiss on the pulse point beneath her ear. "They add a certain something, don't they?"

Her heart, already committed to him beyond everything sensible, contracted. "It's something, all right."

"How about some coffee?" he asked, letting go as he moved into the kitchen.

She was going to need a lot more than coffee, but that would do for a start. "Sure. Did my supplier send over everything for dinner?"

"He did." As she pulled the chicken out of the fridge, Trevor ran his hand over her hip. "According to Fred he seemed pretty possessive of you."

She swung around to the stove. "Fred in security downstairs?" When he nodded, she added, "The relationship between a caterer and her supplier is sacred."

"As long as all he gives you is carrots and potatoes..."

When she trailed her finger down the center of his chest, he tugged her to him. "You keep me pretty satisfied otherwise."

"Do I?"

"Definitely." She kissed his jaw. "But there are miles to go..."

"I know."

Trevor, too, was frustrated with the obstacles that continued to bombard them. Along with trying to get past the secrets they'd kept from each other and the unexpected speed bump of his father's visit, Max was standing in the damn road.

But no matter Max's mistakes, Trevor couldn't help but struggle with the idea of moving against him and siding with a woman he'd known only a few weeks.

He was crazy about Shelby. He craved her presence, her touch, her laugh. She was his lover and friend.

Yet how could he reconcile his actions? How could he turn his back on his family loyalty?

As the chicken cooked, he and Shelby shared coffee at the counter. He told her about his day, and the normalcy of his work helped his mind shift from the turmoil they were going through. By comparison, the complications of logistics, transferring goods from one county, state or country to another, seemed simple.

She shared the silliness of the luncheon she'd catered that afternoon, where the client had asked for a vegetarian menu, only to have several guests complaining about the lack of meat.

"Did you tell them their host had requested the menu?" he asked as the sun descended and the lights of the city flicked on.

"No way. The client is always right, especially this one, who lied through her teeth and said she hadn't requested vegetarian but instead told everyone that I'd bragged about my great produce supplier. I do have one, by the way. But she left out the part where she told me several of her guests couldn't possibly eat flesh." She rolled her eyes. "Though nobody seemed to have a problem with leather bags or shoes."

The thought of Shelby having to apologize for a mistake she hadn't made was maddening. "So you took the blame?"

She shrugged. "She's a good client, and I've gotten plenty of bookings from her friends, too. Rich people are an odd crowd sometimes, but I need them." Her gaze flicked to his. "No offense."

"None taken."

"I also produced a container of chicken salad that I'd made for a just-in-case scenario, and three of the women liked it so much, they ordered several large servings each. In the end, I got future business and was able to add to the client's bill by charging her for something she hadn't ordered but nevertheless saved her party."

"How practical."

"A necessary trait in the food-service business. Especially when the household coffers are as modest as mine."

As soon as the words were out of her mouth, she shook her head. "Sorry." She set down her coffee mug and crossed to the oven, presumably to check on dinner. "I seem determined to point out our differences tonight."

"I understand practicality. I employ it myself every day."

She opened the oven, releasing the mouthwatering scent of roasting chicken into the air. "Every business owner does, I guess…if they want to be successful."

Her spirit was so strong. Her generosity and jaunty attitude a balm to the problem they found themselves mired in.

He hoped his father didn't ruin the mood with what was guaranteed to be harsh judgment on how Trevor was managing Max. He'd stopped asking long ago why the younger had to watch out for the elder. Max was special, after all. The Heir. Not to mention Max wasn't capable of managing to plan his daily meals, much less his entire life.

For a few minutes, they'd been talking about their day like a real couple. Could that become the norm? Could they have a future together?

No easy answers. No simple path.

Weren't the best things in life worth a fight?

"Even my father is practical," he said, rinsing their mugs and placing them in the dishwasher. "Every year around Christmas he'd threaten to turn off the heat if my brother and I didn't stop opening the door every five minutes."

"I imagine Westmore Manor isn't known for its insulation."

"It was built in 1674. Additions and modernizations can only do so much."

"I bet." She cocked her head. "Now that I know you so… intimately, I can't imagine you toiling around a bleak old manor house."

"It's pretty luxurious actually." He gave her a teasing smile. "And not even the servants toiled. And Father put a padlock on the door to the dungeon after he heard me threatening to capture the girl next door."

"To play doctor, I'll bet."

"Certainly not." He put on a face of mock insult. "At the time I wanted to be a solicitor. I couldn't wait to practice my cross-examination techniques."

"Uh-huh. How cute was this girl?"

"Quite." He crossed to her, lifting her onto the counter and moving between her legs. "A redhead as I recall."

"Such good taste at so young an age. I don't have to curtsy when I meet him, do I?"

"My Father? Hell, no." Clearly, he wasn't the only one with more on his mind than dinner and *how-was-your-day-honey?* conversation. He grasped her wrists, gliding her arms around his neck. So normal. So easy. So right. "Frankly, I can't wait to see what the orthodox earl makes of my rebel Yank."

"I hope, for your sake at least, we don't come to blows. He's going to blame you for the mess with Max, isn't he?"

He decided not to answer her question about blame and rile her too soon. "I hope the same—for his sake."

"Fine, so I'll help you pat his hand, assure him everything's peachy with his Number One Son, then ship him back across the ocean so we can get on with our dastardly plan to ruin Max."

Trevor pulled her closer to hide his wince. *Ruin.* He was planning to ruin his own brother.

"You smell really good." She nuzzled his neck, scattering his guilt over Max. "Last week, after you told me to get lost, I bought your cologne to remind me of you."

His heart skipped a beat. "Did you?"

"It made me feel closer to you. Especially since I thought you'd never speak to me again, much less touch me."

He tightened his grip around her waist. Her hips bumped his. Physical need rode high, even as everything between them rose even higher, preventing them from being truly connected. "I'd never have been able to stay away, even if you hadn't come to me."

"Do you feel like we're standing on the edge of something?" she whispered. "It might be great. It might be a disaster."

He hadn't been scared of anything or anyone in a long, long time. But he well remembered the helpless sensation. He couldn't go back.

She braced her hands on either side of his face. "We'll—"

The intercom buzzed. "Mr. Banfield?"

Reluctantly, Trevor let go of Shelby and crossed to the speaker. "Yes?"

"Your guest has arrived," Fred said. "He's coming up in elevator two."

"Thank you."

Trevor took a deep breath, then released it. Was he ready to placate and ultimately lie to the man who'd raised him? A man he loved and respected? All for the greater good?

With a sigh, he headed down the hall. Robin Hood would be so proud.

SHELBY BUSIED HERSELF in the kitchen while Trevor answered the door.

The chicken looked perfect, roasted to a light golden brown, the vegetables scattered around as if a stylist had arranged them for a cookbook photograph. The table was set with white china, silver and sparkling crystal.

Provided she didn't blab out her plans to ruin the future earl, who was, in truth, a creep instead of the respected gentleman he should be, she might survive the night.

As she stripped off her chef's jacket, she heard both men's voices in the hall. They sounded so similar, she couldn't tell whose was whose. She supposed she should have expected the likeness, and the idea made her feel somehow closer to the man who'd sired the man she loved.

But sad at the same time. She and Trevor had a bond, but not a likely future.

As father and son rounded the corner into the kitchen, she blinked. The resemblance didn't stop at the way they sounded.

This is how Trevor will look in twenty-five years.

Well, except for the tweed suit.

"Sir, this is Shelby Dixon," Trevor said.

"Good evening, Lord Westmore. How was your flight?"

"Fine. Thank you." He glanced at his son. "I didn't know you had company. Perhaps we should schedule our meeting for the morning."

Trevor slid his arm around Shelby's waist. "I wanted you to meet Shelby."

The earl's gaze shifted between the two of them. "I see."

Up close, Shelby could see the differences in the two men beyond age. The earl's mouth was smaller, tighter. His eyes weren't as vibrant as Trevor's, and an air of disapproval seemed to emanate from him.

"She's an important part of our discussion." He smiled at her. "And she's a trained chef who offered to make dinner."

"A cook?"

Shelby accepted the earl's appraisal and judgment silently. She'd been too hasty with the thought that they were going to be compatible.

"A chef," Trevor corrected, and Shelby heard the suppressed anger in his tone.

It was gonna be a long, damn night. "Why don't you make you and your father a drink? He looks like a martini kind of guy."

The earl's eyes registered surprise.

"I'll throw together a salad," Shelby finished.

Trevor slid his hand up her back, a silent gesture of support, then escorted his father into the living room.

"Trevor, it looks like the botanical gardens in here. Don't you have a cleaning service?"

Shelby rolled her eyes and headed for the fridge. She hoped her supplier had sent the wine she'd ordered. She opened the bottle of premium chardonnay and poured a healthy glass. With Trevor's budget, she'd splurged, and the reward in taste and quality was well worth it.

If she and Trevor had been dating six months, if she wasn't half out of her mind with worry for her parents, if she wasn't hell-bent on vengeance against the great and wonderful heir, if, in other words, they were a regular couple, maybe they'd have a chance at a real relationship. Maybe his dad's appearance wouldn't be so difficult. She wouldn't feel so vulnerable and defensive at the same time.

She chopped salad ingredients and tossed them with fresh varieties of lettuce. She set both the salad bowl and her half-full wineglass in the fridge.

She was going to need all her wits about her to get through dinner.

When she walked into the living room, tension lay as thick as the low-lying clouds outside the windows. A storm was brewing—both indoors and out.

Both men stood as she entered. Their manners were as engrained as their DNA, after all.

"Would you like a drink?" Trevor asked as he approached her.

"No, thanks." She looked into the clear blue of his eyes and leaned into his caress across her cheek. "I'm good."

They sat on the sofa with Trevor between his father and her, and the earl caught up his son on the news in London and at the manor. It was generally a list of names and accomplishments, hirings and firings, births and deaths, but there was a moment or two when a twinkle appeared in the earl's eyes, and the charm that had developed fully in his son was evident.

During dinner, the polite conversation continued. No mention of Max the Swindler or the fact that Trevor was sleeping with a woman considered a mere domestic. The earl was politely complimentary of the food, but since bland roast beef and potatoes were the benchmark, Shelby didn't take offense.

After polishing off a dessert of peach cobbler, which Pops ate every crumb of, the earl pushed back his chair and rose. "I suppose you're wondering what brought me here so unexpectedly."

Seeming calm, Trevor sipped coffee. But Shelby knew his expressions well. He was bracing himself.

"I assume you're here because of the publicity Max has been getting lately," he said.

"I thought you had the situation here under control, Trevor." The earl's hands, resting at his sides, curled into fists, and the temperature in the room dropped at least twenty degrees. "But obviously I was mistaken about the seriousness with which you regard your family. I'm here because a New York police detective called me to ask if I was aware a woman had filed a complaint against my son for fraud and did I have a comment on those potential charges."

The earl's eyes turned to ice. "Would *you* care to comment, Trevor?"

14

SHELBY SUCKED IN A shocked gulp of air.

She wanted to reach across the table and grab Trevor's hand, but his stoney expression stopped her.

Antonio? What the hell was he doing? Why was he interfering again? Supposedly oh-so-busy following her and her friends in addition to his East River homicide, he must have found a vacant spot on his crowded calendar.

The earl opened and closed his hands in silent condemnation, as he apparently struggled to gather his temper. "What are these lies about fraud and nonsense? You told me you had Max under control, Trevor." He braced his hand on the table as he leaned toward his son. "What if this gets out? The tabloids are ruthless."

Guess he hadn't struggled too hard.

"We have a lot more to worry about than the press, sir," Trevor said stoically. "The suspicion of fraud isn't a lie."

Shelby goggled at Trevor. Why wasn't he defending himself? He was supposed to keep Max under control? What a joke.

"Max isn't merely overextending himself or investing in businesses without preparation," Trevor continued. "He's actively swindling people."

The earl's face turned stark white. "He's not. He can't be."

Resignation in every line of his body, Trevor rose. "He is."

Shelby remained rooted to her chair. Even with the earl's nasty attitude, she knew it couldn't be easy to hear his child was a crook.

"The woman Detective Antonio referred to is one victim," Trevor explained. "Shelby's parents are another. And there are more."

The earl glanced at Shelby, then dismissed her just as quickly, and she felt less sorry for him. "How could he have gotten himself into anything illegal? I thought you were watching him."

"I can't follow him around every minute," Trevor returned. "And he got himself into this mess. I've tried to help him, tried to counsel him. On your orders, I've bailed him out of debt and scandal. No matter what, he keeps falling."

"Ridiculous." The earl lifted his chin. "He's a Banfield. His bloodline is impeccable, his future secure. Obviously you're not doing enough, or things would not have progressed to this level. Can you talk to the detective? Keep this development quiet?"

"This development is an illegal investment scam." Trevor's tone rose in disbelief. "He stole money from decent, hard-working people."

The earl shifted his gaze to Shelby. "According to *your* parents, I suppose. And yet you seem quite close to my other son. How…convenient."

"Convenient?" Rage coursed through Shelby as she surged to her feet. "Look here, buddy, I'm—"

Trevor grabbed her hand, giving it a long squeeze. "Shelby, please."

Tears clogged the back of her throat as she watched the struggle in every line of Trevor's body. Love welled up in her, taking her breath.

Her revenge wasn't for her alone anymore. It wasn't a furious impulse, or an act of desperation. She needed to end Max's schemes for her parents, for the other victims and definitely for Trevor. The blame he bore was misplaced.

She nodded and let go of his hand, though she remained standing, anticipating the next blow.

"I have talked to the detective, sir," Trevor said in an amazingly composed tone. "He's busy doing his job, not giving press interviews. But that's hardly—"

"While you're distracted with your bedmate, our family name is fodder for the gossipmongers. Do you know how that makes me look? Do you understand the ramifications for your brother's reputation? Do you care at all for the ancient and revered name you were blessed to be born with?" He jabbed his finger against the dining table. "Fix it."

The muscle along Trevor's jaw pulsed.

Shelby dearly hoped he didn't grind his beautiful teeth to dust.

"I'm doing my best," Trevor managed to say. "You didn't need to come all the way here and reprimand me like a five-year-old."

Disbelief radiated from the earl. "Is that what you've learned in America, disrespect for your father?"

Okay, that's it.

She didn't want to embarrass Trevor, but she was done being bullied by this pompous, overbearing *gentleman.* She marched around the table and stood nearly toe-to-toe with the earl. "Why is it Trevor's responsibility to handle Max? He's a grown man. It seems to me that if everybody *stopped* handling him, he'd be where he belongs—jail."

The earl's face turned an alarming shade of red. "The future Earl of Banfield incarcerated? Young woman, you cannot possibly understand the ramifications of that outcome."

"Sure I do." Shelby crossed her arms over her chest. "Every

family has some relative who stole a car, or went streaking through the quad during college or drinks too much and hollers at the TV newscasters. For the Dixons it's my crazy uncle Larry, who spends half the day sitting in a lawn chair under his carport sniffing paint thinner."

Trevor smiled. His father looked horrified.

And Shelby felt much better. "A couple of years in prison might do Max a world of good. It would surely be cheaper for you two. Plus, when he gets out—all freshly rehabilitated—you can plan a great public relations campaign. Second Chance for Wayward Heir. A friend of mine works for the best PR firm in the city. She'll fix you up."

Trevor, used to her outspokenness, looked interested by her spin on the the situation, which made her feel less guilty, as well. Max deserved to pay for his crimes, but he wasn't an evil psychopath. A little time behind bars might be the tough love he needed.

By contrast, the earl appeared incapable of speech. Which was surprising. With a kid like Max, Shelby had figured him for an expert in hostile communications.

"The press is hardly our biggest concern, sir," Trevor said. "He's going to need a good lawyer."

"It won't come to that," the earl insisted.

Good grief. Did delusion run in the family? The man insisted Trevor manage Max's life and mistakes, but didn't trust his judgment?

"Regardless," the earl continued haughtily, "I'm sure Trevor has the funds to recover the Dixon family's losses."

Trevor's body jerked as if he'd been struck. "You don't know Shelby, sir," he said slowly. "Because I'm certain if you did, you'd greatly regret insulting her integrity."

Shelby didn't flinch from the earl's jibe. He was, after all, doing exactly what she was—protecting his family. He also didn't realize just how personally she was taking that quest.

Just as she was determined to bring Max to justice, he'd no doubt do everything in his power to keep her and Trevor apart once Project Robin Hood's secrets came out.

Still, she wasn't deterred. "And if you knew me really well, you'd know it isn't wise to come between me and something I want."

TREVOR FOUND HER SITTING on the chaise longue, scowling at the trees.

"I'm sorry I spoke to him like that," she said, not sounding sorry at all.

After her warning to his father, she'd stormed up the stairs to the terrace. He'd let her go, knowing she needed to cool off.

Surprisingly, his father hadn't commented on her abrupt exit or the confrontation over Max. He'd simply thanked him for dinner and left for his hotel.

Not sure how much time to give her, and definitely not wanting to be added to the growing list of Banfields she'd like to slug, Trevor had cleaned up the dessert plates and cups.

The caffeine and tense conversation had him wired, so he wandered around the living room for a few minutes before spotting a particularly pretty pansy. Snapping off the blossom, he'd twirled it between his fingers as he mounted the stairs. Just when he thought they'd found some common ground, the world tilted sideways.

"How many years in prison would I get if I punched out a cop?" she asked.

"Quite a few, I'd imagine."

"How about English nobility?"

"Would you rather if I'd done more to defend you?"

Her eyes fired as she stared hard at him. "I can fight my own battles."

"But you don't have to fight them alone, and I'm not the enemy." He handed her the pansy blossom. "I come in peace."

She brought it to her lips. "Thanks. They're edible, you know."

He hadn't brought it for her to eat. Maybe he should have given her more time and space. Or more flowers. Still, beneath her anger and defensiveness, she was hurting, and he wanted to be there to comfort her as long as she was down.

He sat on the end of the chaise. "If you glare at the trees like that the leaves are going to fall off."

"What the devil do you know about horticulture?"

"Obviously less than I do about comforting my girlfriend."

Surprise forced the irritated lines from her forehead. She raised her eyebrows. "Girlfriend?"

He'd let the word slip, though it was true. But now didn't seem like the opportune time for that discussion. "Problem?"

"No." With a sigh, she scooted next to him and laid her head against his shoulder. "I really am sorry I argued with your father."

"You shouldn't be. You were right. And, he started it."

"Maybe he's still bitter about us kicking his butt at Yorktown."

Laughing, he pulled her onto his lap. "I wouldn't entirely rule that out." He kissed her softly, feeling the tension drain from her body. Finally, he was getting the hang of comfort. "We made a good team tonight."

"You controlled your temper better than I did."

"I have more experience."

"Does he think I'm an ill-mannered lout?"

He kissed the underside of her jaw. "If he does, he didn't say so."

"Did he tell you to dump me?"

"No, and I wouldn't even if he did. I don't take orders from him."

"Except when it comes to Max."

Irritation rolled over him. He might have been furious—if she wasn't right. "Not anymore. I'm on your side, remember?"

She stroked his face with the pansy. "I don't want anybody taking sides. Max shouldn't come between you and your father. And neither should I."

"Don't worry about it."

"But—"

"Max started this, not you."

She searched his gaze, her eyes filled with anxiety and determination, the same emotions that churned in his stomach. "And we're going to finish it?"

"We are." He skimmed his mouth across her cheek. "In the meantime, I know how you can support me."

"Remember you're not alone, either."

"As it happens the kind of comforting I have in mind is best done in pairs."

Project Robin Hood, Day 24
Paddy's Bar

"HAVE YOU LOST YOUR mind?" Calla demanded as she slid onto the barstool next to Detective Antonio. "Why'd you call Trevor's father?"

Pausing with a beer bottle halfway to his mouth, the detective scowled. "Why are you always bothering me?"

"I live to be annoying. A trait you ought to be familiar with."

"What'll ya have?" the burly bartender asked.

Calla noticed most the patrons around her were enjoying beer or amber-colored liquids. Asking for a diet soda would probably get her tossed out on her butt, but dear heaven it was barely noon. "I'll have what he's having," she said, flicking her thumb toward Antonio.

"How did you find me?"

She glanced around the rustic, Irish-themed tavern. There were more cops than shamrocks in the joint. "This place is across the street from your precinct house. I took a wild guess. What are you doing in here in the middle of the day?"

"I pulled an all-nighter and just got off shift. Are you my mother now?"

"You could use some guidance and discipline," she muttered, then took a sip of her beer. Grimacing, she set it down. "Why did you call Lord Westmore?"

"Hello? You people are the ones butting into my case, doing my surveillance. I figured you'd appreciate me trying to shake things up. Somebody or something's got to break."

"But we have a plan, and you're going to screw it up. We're trying to be low-key here. If the earl tells Max you called, he's going to hop out of here like a rabbit with his cottontail on fire."

Antonio blinked. "A rabbit with his—" He stopped and shook his head, as if the reference were too ridiculous to analyze. "Is the earl going to tell Max?"

"No. Trevor met with him this morning and asked him not to. Shelby says the earl doesn't believe Max has done anything illegal."

"Then what's the big deal?" He took a long swallow of beer. "And what plan do you have? You chicks need to stay out of this case and let me do my job."

"Chicks? This isn't a farm. We're women—and best friends besides—and we're gonna do what we have to in order to put that slimeball out of commission."

Antonio leaned toward her. Their faces were bare inches apart. She could see golden flecks in his deep green eyes. "What plan?"

The man was the most contentious, aggravating, bossy... sexier-than-sin— She stopped her internal tirade and cleared her throat. "We're still considering our options."

"Hell." He polished off his beer and laid some money on the bar. "See ya, Jimmie," he called to the bartender.

"Where're you going?" she asked. She'd come to scold him. A lot of nerve he had not to even stick around for her censure.

"Home. To bed."

A vision of his rumpled dark hair and naked, leanly muscled body tangled in soft cotton sheets wavered before her. She grabbed the bar to steady herself before calling after him. "You could help, you know."

He barked out a laugh. "Under your direction."

"Naturally."

"No, thanks."

"Shel, there's a guy named Henry Banfield out here to see you."

Elbow deep in floured dough, Shelby glanced toward Pete, hovering in the doorway between the front office and the workroom. "There is?"

"Yep." Pete angled his head. "Trevor's father?"

"Uh-huh."

"Uh-oh."

Shelby put on a brave smile, though her stomach was rapidly tying itself in knots.

Pete kept the bills paid and answered phones a few days a week in between classes at NYU. Someday, he'd be a brilliant accountant. She felt fortunate to have his good sense on the payroll.

"Send him on back."

"I could tell him you're busy."

"No." She headed to the sink to wash her hands. She couldn't imagine whatever the earl had to say would be encouraging, but she didn't see how delaying the confrontation would help. "I'll see him."

"Okay. I'm gonna transfer the phones back here and take off. I've got a world-history midterm tomorrow."

"Yeah, sure. Thanks, Pete."

She heard voices in the front room, then Lord Westmore entered the room.

Dressed in a tailor-made charcoal-gray suit—not tweed— he looked more like his son than ever.

Shelby swallowed the lump in her throat as she dried her hands. "Good afternoon, your lordship. What can I do for you?"

His hands clasped behind his back, he wandered around the room, pausing at the stove top. "Chicken soup?" he asked.

"Just chicken," she said, wondering where this was going. Was he casing the joint or assessing its value? Either way, she doubted the earl had troubled himself to come to her kitchen to chat about culinary endeavors. "I'm making chicken pot-pies for a charity luncheon tomorrow."

"Really?" He actually smiled. "I enjoy a good chicken potpie."

"Do you?"

"Though I'm especially partial to roasted beef."

"Trevor mentioned that."

"He thought the meal was dull. But I like tradition."

"My mom made grilled-cheese sandwiches every Tuesday night when I was growing up. 'Course, that was probably be-cause it was the only thing she knew how to make without burning the house down." She halted the urge to continue rambling. "Were you expecting to find Trevor here?"

"No, I came at this time because I know he's at his office." He stopped on the opposite side of the center island. "You and my son have become quite close recently."

Then again, maybe she'd rather talk about food. "We have."

"You met when you catered a party for Max."

"That's right."

"A party you and your friends used to garner information about Max and his allegedly illicit business ventures."

She braced her hands against the counter. *Yes, it started with a lie. Thanks for the reminder.* "Do you have a point, your lordship?"

His gaze met hers. "You're very direct. You remind me of my former wife. Different coloring, of course, but full of fire and independence. You know what you want."

"Yes."

"But you're not capricious and unreliable."

"No."

"And right now you want my son?"

Shelby pursed her lips. "It took you quite a while to get around to that."

His face flushed. "I have difficulties communicating with women at times."

"We're all just a little bit different," Shelby said sardonically. "It must be frustrating."

"Simply maddening."

"So you came here to find out if I'm using him? For his rich friends as potential clients or the luxury of sleeping in his high-rise apartment?"

"Maybe both."

"With his looks and success I imagine he's caught the attention of a number of women who're interested in the... Let's call them *benefits* that come with being involved with him."

"Yes, he has."

"Did you warn them off, too?"

"Sometimes."

"Sorry, my lord, but, as they say in my neck of the woods, *that dog won't hunt* here."

Looking resigned, he nodded. "I was afraid of that."

Though she didn't have to like it, she understood his suspicion. A father should safeguard his son—even if he's the second, just-in-case one—like a daughter should honor her parents. They were alike in more ways than either of them wanted to admit. "As much as I long to tell you that my relationship with Trevor is none of your damn business, I'm aware your intent is to protect him."

"He cares for you very much."

"I feel the same. He's already offered me money for my parents. I won't take it."

"Not yet."

She shook her head. "Not ever."

After holding her gaze a long moment, he again nodded. "I believe you." He paced the length of the island, then back. "And I misjudged you." He shrugged. "It happens, though I like to think not often. There was my wife…" He trailed off. "But then I have Max and Trevor, so I can hardly call the relationship a mistake.

"I was young and impulsive—hard as that may be to believe now."

"It is."

"Perhaps I learned from my mistakes. Or lost my nerve. But family obligations, and the title, require a decorum Trevor isn't burdened with. He has more freedoms. I imagine that's why he chose to live in America. As a result he's done more with less."

"You might try telling him this. He needs to hear it."

"Yes, well, we need to get through this Max business. Do you really think he deserves to go to jail?"

"At the very least."

The earl sighed. "Bloody Americans, bent on retribution."

"You *are* still pissed about us kicking your butt at Yorktown."

He chuckled, and the humor made her ache for Trevor all the more. She was crazy about that smile, and the events of the next few days were likely to determine how often she might get to see it in the future. "Are you aware my ancestor led the attack?" he asked.

"And got his butt kicked."

He inclined his head, the elegance of the gesture certainly genetic as she'd seen her lover do the same thing many times. "I hope you make him happy."

"Me, too."

"Do you love him?"

"Yes."

She'd answered instinctively, probably rashly, but she couldn't regret the truth. There were too many deceptions, slights and injustices already.

"Have you told him?"

"No."

"Don't wait. Trevor deserves to be happy, and I think you do that very well."

She thought so—for now anyway. The lies and the plots were incredible obstacles to overcome however. When the business with Max was over, would she always be a reminder of his brother's downfall? And what if they didn't get enough evidence to have him arrested? Would she grow to resent Trevor?

"As long as we're sharing confidences," the earl added, "I should admit there are times I wish Trevor could have been my firstborn and heir. If the birth order had simply been reversed."

Wishing for something impossible to change seemed like a giant waste of time to Shelby. "Why does birth order matter?"

"It does" was all he said.

But if Max went to jail, couldn't he be disinherited? She didn't know how that kind of thing worked in the U.K., but with enough political and legal wrangling, she imagined anything was possible.

"Trevor would make an excellent earl," Shelby agreed.

As the words escaped her lips, fear surged through her. What if that happened?

He would have a seat in the House of Important Noble People, or whatever they called it. He'd have to go back to England. His wife would be a *countess*.

She wasn't countess material.

And even without the title, he was still British nobility, and she was a caterer. He moved goods back and forth around the world; she boxed cupcakes and sold them to the neighborhood coffee shops.

She was a fool to think she could hold on to the man she loved so deeply.

The earl crossed to the stove, lifted the stock pot lid and inhaled. "You're an excellent cook." He glanced at her over his shoulder, and she fought to focus on him instead of the dread slithering through her veins like poison. "Sorry. It's *chef*, isn't it? I expect you can make lemonade quite easily."

"Lemons and sugar."

"I'll leave that to you."

The metaphor between her and Trevor's relationship, making something good and sweet out of something that started bitter wasn't lost on her.

But it didn't give her the hope the earl undoubtedly intended.

"So, during my meeting this morning with Trevor," the earl continued, "after viewing the evidence compiled against Max, it occurred to me that my burden on Trevor has been too great. I realized I could assist instead of order or criticize. So what exactly goes into making a chicken potpie?"

15

Trevor walked into a scene in Shelby's catering kitchen that caused him to come to a halt in the doorway.

His father was wearing an apron and stirring something on the stove. Calla and Victoria were sitting side by side on the counter. Each had a plastic bowl in their lap and flour on their hands. Shelby was dipping a ladle into a pitcher that looked remarkably like lemonade.

He blinked at the homey atmosphere. Something was really wrong and really right.

Father is wearing an apron.

That was probably the wrong thing.

"You're having a party and didn't invite me?" he asked, entering the room.

"We made lemonade," his father said with a joy on his face Trevor had only seen a few times in his life.

Calla toasted him with a V-shaped crystal glass. "And lemon-drop martinis."

"Chicken-pot pies have been promised," Victoria said in her usual dry tone. "If Henry will get a move on over there…"

"Henry?" Trevor managed to echo.

Shelby put down the ladle she was holding and closed the distance between them. "Hey."

Just that quickly, the world narrowed to two. He braced his hands on either side of her waist. "Everything okay?"

"We've had our strange moments."

"Was one of those tying an apron around the lofty Earl of Westmore's waist?"

"Oh, yeah. He got through it."

"And you?"

"I'm great." Though there was a hint of tension in her smile, she moved closer, brushing her lips across his cheek. "Even better now."

"*Aw,* look how cute they are," Calla said.

Shelby grinned. "Calla's had two lemon drops already."

Trevor pulled Shelby tight into his embrace. It was like coming home, only better. His kissed the top of her head. "I can tell."

Desire crawled through his veins as she loosened his tie, sliding it from around his neck and looping it around hers like a scarf. She linked their hands. "Come join us."

He'd thrown himself in with Robin Hood and her compatriots. He supposed it was time for some merriment.

Though there was also hard work—stirring, chopping, kneading, rolling, scooping. With the potpies for Shelby's luncheon stored in the walk-in fridge, the gang was left to make their dinner.

Unable to face a potpie after all the ones they'd slaved over, they formed dumplings from leftover dough and added chicken and vegetables. They poured fresh stock, thickened with flour for the broth. Shelby directed his father on how to make a loaf of herbed bread, and Trevor opened the wine.

Gathered in folding chairs in the back corner of the kitchen, they feasted. Not even a party in Sherwood Forest could have competed.

"I don't want to ruin the mood," Trevor said, "but we need to talk about Max."

Victoria groaned. "How 'bout I just run over the creep the next time I'm following him?"

When the earl's face registered shock, Shelby patted his hand. "Sorry, Henry. Victoria's even more direct than I am."

"Quite all right, my dear." The earl offered her a slight smile. "Max can't continue hurting people. He has to change his life. The Banfield name is at stake."

Ever since their talk that morning, Trevor was finding his father's change of heart a little unnerving. He appreciated the earl not warning Max of the forces moving against him, but he wasn't sure how to take his father's active involvement in the Robin Hood project.

The fact that, apparently, it came down to the family reputation shouldn't have been so surprising. It was also entirely possible the old man was as pissed off at Max as Trevor was.

Calla frowned into her water glass. "Detective Antonio is out of patience with us. If we're not careful, we'll be the ones behind bars."

"I think we're all tired and frustrated," Trevor said. "We need to expose Max's crimes and end this."

"We need a better plan than the last time we confronted Max," Shelby pointed out.

"I've been giving that some thought," Trevor said. "How about if we're honest?"

Victoria gestured with her fork. "I'd bet my Mercedes Max knows zero about honesty. It's worked pretty well for him so far."

Trevor sipped his wine. "Well, we won't be telling him everything. Just enough to lure him into our trap."

"Which is?" Shelby asked.

"We're not having any luck contacting anybody from the investors' meeting or finding proof of defrauded victims Shelby hasn't already documented, so what if we're the fresh evidence? What if we go with Shelby's original idea and become Max's next mark?"

"We, as in all of us?" Calla asked, glancing around the table and looking doubtful.

"We'll plan everything together, but I think we need one investor, and I have the perfect woman in mind."

Everyone fell silent as they all looked to Shelby for her reaction.

"I'm fine with being the would-be victim," she said. "I think I'd enjoy the end result all the more. But how? Do I pull out the blond wig and false eyelashes again?"

Victoria frowned. "I vote no on that part."

"I wasn't thinking of Shelby actually," Trevor explained quickly before they ran full tilt with costume ideas. "How about my administrative assistant?"

"Florence?" the earl and Shelby asked at the same time and in the same disbelieving tone.

Trevor tried not to take their reaction as criticism. "Yes, Florence. Max was at school when she was my governess, and only met her a few times. She recently came out of retirement to work for me, and Max hasn't ever bothered to come to my office here in New York. He won't recognize her, and more importantly we can trust her.

"I'll bring her to the next investors' meeting, and we'll say she has family money she wants to invest in one of the new condos. Simple. He'll trust us, because he'd never dream I'd betray him. I've invested too much effort into bailing him out of trouble."

Shelby cocked her head in confusion. "Does Florence have family money?"

"Does she need the actual cash?" Calla asked. "Why not just say she does? He gave you a bad check. Let's return the favor."

"I think the money should be real for this to work," Shelby

said. "If he cashes the check and it clears, won't that be stronger evidence for the police? A paper trail?"

"Hold on." Trevor scowled at Shelby. "What bad check?"

"Sorry," Calla said, shoving a bite of bread in her mouth and looking guilty.

"The check from Max for my catering services at the hotel," Shelby admitted. "It bounced."

Trevor ground his teeth together. "You have to let me—"

"No, I don't." Shelby shook her head. "I knew the risk of him stiffing me going in. It was my decision to go ahead anyway."

"There's an easy solution to the problem of the money," Victoria said, "I've got plenty—"

Shelby waved her off. "No. It's too big of a risk."

"*I'm* giving Florence the money," Trevor said firmly.

Shelby narrowed her eyes. "Oh, no you're not. We're not using your money, either."

Trevor laid his hand on her thigh, squeezing it lightly to calm and reassure her. "She'll be borrowing it to get to Max."

"Unless he takes off before we can get him arrested." Her expression was mutinous. "And I don't like dragging Florence into this. I'll be the mark."

"Florence doesn't mind," Trevor insisted. "Trust me, she'll enjoy the adventure."

Shelby seemed on the verge of offering another excuse when Calla said, "If you're the mark, Trevor will have to deposit the investment into your bank account."

Shelby's face turned white. "No. He can't."

The earl abruptly covered Shelby's hand with his. "This isn't what I meant earlier."

She focused on him. "I know."

While Trevor, and presumably the other women, remained confused, his father added, "How about if you use my money?"

"No way." Shelby jerked to her feet, tossing her napkin on the table. "I appreciate everybody's help, I really do, but all of you are spending way too much time and energy on this. I'll keep researching and looking for people willing to give statements to the police. There'll be no more surveillance or break-ins or any of it. I can do this."

"On your own?" Victoria finished for her.

"That's not fair," Calla said. "We want revenge as much as you do. It's not right what Max is doing."

"You need us," Trevor said, his voice tight with disappointment. Why wouldn't she trust them? Him especially? The ache in his heart spread. He loved her, and she was rejecting him.

"Let your friends help, Shelby," the earl said quietly. "They want to share in the responsibility."

"Shelby, why don't you come to the meeting, too?" Trevor suggested. "You can pose as Florence's daughter or niece, maybe her secretary. You'll be right there to make sure nothing goes wrong."

Shelby stood rigid, and Trevor fought for the words that would convince her. *All for one, and one for all?*

Oh, wait. That was *The Three Musketeers.*

Tentatively, Calla raised her hand. "I could use some extra cash. Any of you guys want to deposit a big, heaping pile of it in my bank account, I'm cool with that."

Her silly offer broke the tension.

"Okay. Hell." Shelby looked skyward, then dropped into her seat. "We'll do it. It's a good plan." Under the table, she laced her fingers through Trevor's. "But Max is already suspicious of you. You questioned him about his CD investment, and he knows you're watching him. What if he senses the trap?"

"He'll take off like a jackrabbit," Calla said.

Victoria drummed her fingers against the table. "We've come too far to risk spooking him now."

"What if I escort Shelby and Florence to the investment meeting?" the earl offered.

Before Trevor could be little more than shocked by his father's offer, he continued. "Naturally, he won't suspect me of trapping him."

"Are you sure you want to be that involved?" Trevor asked his father.

"Love isn't always easy, son," the earl said, resignation in his eyes. "I want to be there."

"Provided your sudden appearance doesn't scare him to death," Victoria said drily.

"He won't be scared," Trevor said, certain it was true.

Having his powerful father there would make Max bolder than ever. After seeing his brother through Shelby's eyes, he'd gained a bit of insight into his character just as she had. Max would puff up like one of the hot-air balloons he was now notorious for wanting to buy.

Trevor exchanged a meaningful glance with Shelby, who nodded. "I think it could work."

All for one.

Condos for Sale!
by Peeps Galloway, Gossipmonger
(And proud of it!)

On guard, fellow Manhattanites!

Did you hear one of our beloved avant-garde artistes in the East Village has gone on to that great Picasso painting in the sky? Yes, I know, let us all shed a tear into our whiskey sour. (Which is *the* hot drink of spring, by the by.) He will never be forgotten by all who cherished his groundbreaking work.

But we all must go on...on to the real-estate section of this quality publication, as an oh-so-discreet ad for a new condominium development has been placed. (See pgs. 9 and 10 for the full-color spread.) Through a delightful real-estate agent named Alice, you, too, can get all the deets on the budding project. And even get in on the ground floor of what's sure to be Manhattan's new IT address!

One scoop you won't get from the lovely Alice, though, is the brainchild behind this development. (You know I know, and you know I'm going to let you know. 'Cause, you know, we're buds.) It's Max Banfield! Imagine our very own, newly crowned hotel mogul and future earl already branching out to other ventures! It makes a shoe diva proud, doesn't it?

Apparently those stories of trouble over at the Crown were greatly exaggerated. Who would start such an unsubstantiated rumor? The nerve of some people.

(For a list of my own sources, please present yourself to 700 Pennsylvania Ave, Wash, D.C., and check out that charming old document under glass called The Constitution. Amendment number one is a doozy.)

Be sure and invite me over for a cocktail when you move into your new lush pad!

—*Peeps*

Project Robin Hood, Day 26
The Crown Jewel, Suite 1634

SHELBY POSITIONED HERSELF behind Henry and Florence as they rode up in the elevator.

"Relax," he said, glancing at her over his shoulder. "It'll be over soon."

She nodded, but her thoughts drifted back to the last time she'd been in this building, when the betrayed look on Trevor's face as he'd confronted her in her ridiculous disguise forced her to admit her plot against Max.

Much had changed; some couldn't be altered.

Deception had dominated her relationship with Trevor. How could anything honest and true bloom from that sad beginning? How could chemistry and a bond over a selfish crook form the basis of love? How would their differences in upbringing, income and status ever merge?

"Let him come to you," Victoria said, her voice coming through courtesy of the tiny earpiece Shelby and the others wore.

Jerking back to reality, Shelby drew deep breaths as she watched the elevator's lit numbers advance higher and higher.

"Don't fidget," Florence whispered, turning to stare at her.

She'd probably said the same thing a thousand times to Trevor in church while he was growing up.

Appreciating the confidence in Florence's sturdy frame and kind brown eyes, Shelby nevertheless shook her head. "I'm supposed to be the mousy niece who keeps track of the checkbook. I'll be more convincing if I twitch."

"We need to make a copy of our small film for an awards committee as well as the police," the secretary said matter-of-factly.

When Shelby frowned, she added, "You're quaking like a sparrow caught in a hurricane."

Annoyed at herself, Shelby rolled her shoulders, pleased to discover her spine was still in place. She wasn't afraid of Max nearly as much as what would happen once he was out of the way, and she and Trevor had to face the unlikely event of their relationship continuing.

"The earpiece works quite well," Henry commented. "Maybe I should get one of these systems for Hastings."

"Hastings?" Shelby asked.

"My house manager," the earl said.

Shelby pictured a stern-faced, gray-haired butler in a three piece black suit. She was so out of her league with these people.

She also had no idea where her friends had gotten the surveillance equipment, complete with an audio bug in Shelby's ring and a mini camera hidden in the arrow-shaped charm around her neck. Or why they felt such extreme measures were necessary. But she expected they'd enjoyed the intrigue.

At least somebody was having fun.

The triumph and anticipation she should feel wasn't there. Anxiety and dread were, however, present in great supply.

"Remember I'm with you," Trevor said, via the same earphone. "You can do this."

Shelby closed her eyes briefly and took a deep breath. Though not near her physically, her lover was manning the recording equipment in a rented hotel suite. Victoria was already at the investors' meeting posing as a potential victim. Calla was in a rented van outside, prepared to follow Max when he left.

What could go wrong?

As Henry and Florence strolled into the suite with her shuffling along behind, she noted everything was set up like the previous gathering, though with a few prosperous additions. The slide show was now accented by a physical model of the building once it was developed into condos. The food table was more opulent and included an ice sculpture in the shape of a swan. The room was more crowded, and the attendees more affluent.

Max had been working hard.

They'd barely crossed the threshold when a waiter offered Florence and Henry glasses of champagne. She was ignored.

Perfect. Not only did she have no intention of toasting anything, Shelby would be most effective if she wasn't memorable.

Henry urged their trio toward the model encased in a glass display. The prospective condo building was a ten-story tower of glass and stone. Tiny trees and people dotted the sidewalks. A park, complete with potted flowers, iron benches and playground equipment, set off the east end of the property.

"It's perfectly peaceful," she said quietly.

"Appearances can be deceptive, my dear," Henry said, smiling at her.

"It's a facade," Florence added.

"It certainly is," Shelby agreed.

"Your lordship."

Careful to keep her face angled downward, Shelby turned as Henry did toward the man with the worshipful voice. Max, naturally.

Through her large, dark-rimmed glasses, she looked past her lanky brown bangs and noticed the scumbag's widened eyes as if he'd been presented with a plate of diamonds. "Father, you're here."

"I am," Henry said, shaking his son's hand, his tone warm but not overdoing it. "I popped into town to see you and Trevor, and he told me about your project. I wanted to see you, naturally, and I thought my friend Florence might be interested."

Florence shook Max's hand as Henry introduced them. Shelby was pointed out as Florence's *quite efficient* niece, Rosemary.

Shelby waited for recognition. She held tight to the leather portfolio she'd brought both as a prop and a place to store Florence's all-important checkbook. Surely they'd all be denounced as frauds.

But Max barely glanced at her—all his attention was for his father and his friend.

"She's going to love this development," Max said, all smiles and welcome. "Let me show you around."

He dragged them from one end of the room to the other, introducing them—well, mainly the earl—to everyone in sight. Shelby finally understood the fawning, false as it might be, that Trevor had endured through his life. Grown people, supposedly independent-thinking Americans who elected their leaders instead of birthing them, fell over Henry like a prince. It was ridiculous and embarrassing.

She'd been somewhat anxious about meeting the earl. While her concern had mostly been over meeting the father of the man she loved, intimidation over the title had come into play. The fact that he lived in a social and economic structure beyond her realm couldn't be ignored. Celebrities were worshipped; teachers were underpaid.

Wasn't that what the Robin Hood legend had been all about? The balance of nobility and greed. The divide between have and have-not. The compulsion to give and take.

And, for her, the desire to resolve injustice.

Through the whole ordeal, Trevor sent encouraging advice through her earpiece and Victoria kept a distant eye on their progress around the room.

Shelby was wrapped in the embrace of her friends, and she'd never felt so comforted—and so afraid of what would happen when they let go.

"It's so beautiful," Florence said, gazing with fake rapture at the slide show Max provided. "I'd love to live there."

"But you can," Max said, his voice low and coaxing. "A committed deposit, and all this can be yours."

Shelby felt Henry's hand press into her back. "A committed deposit of what?" she asked Max.

"Twenty grand," he said, not looking at her at all but Florence. "That's all I need."

It was considerably less than they thought he'd want and much more than she wanted to give. But then she wouldn't willingly give the man cab fare.

Which is probably why, after she wrote a check to Maxwell Banfield Incorporated, her hand jerked as if in protest when she extended it toward her "aunt" to sign.

"Do it," Calla said in her ear.

"End it," Trevor added.

Shelby handed over the check.

Was she ending one crisis only to have her heart broken? How could she and Trevor take what was begun with lies and make magic?

She was fresh out of lemonade.

"DO YOU THINK HE'LL cash the check?"

With Shelby's head resting on his chest, her bare thigh slung over his as they snuggled in his bed, the last thing on earth Trevor wanted to do was talk about Max.

"He'd be silly to cash a check that large. The bank has to file a report of any single withdrawal of more than ten thousand dollars." He stroked her bare back with the tips of his fingers. "Still, he'll probably run to the bank in the morning, even though it's Saturday. The key is where he deposits it. The money should be held in an escrow account reserved for the condo construction."

She pressed her lips against his skin. "And you don't think he'll do that?"

He closed his eyes and fought to concentrate on the question. "I don't think he can spell escrow."

"You're sure your friend at the bank will call when Max comes in?"

"Yes."

"And if he withdraws the money?"

"Then, too. Stop worrying."

"You're the one who should be worrying. It's your money."

"I'll get it back."

She sighed. "My stomach's in knots. How does Detective Antonio do this everyday? I'd go crazy."

"He doesn't have a personal stake in his cases."

"True."

Another kiss to Trevor's chest, and he grinned. He knew she needed to talk through her concerns, but damn it was hard.

"He didn't recognize me," she said softly.

His heart jumped. "Antonio? When did you—"

"No, no." She patted his shoulder. "See, I'm not the only one who's worried."

He tightened his hold on her. He wasn't troubled, per se. Just anxious to end all this intrigue. He had quite a lot to say to Shelby, and he wanted her untroubled and happy when he did.

"Max," she continued. "He didn't recognize me as the caterer from the party. He didn't recognize Florence or suspect his own father had turned on him."

"Did you expect him to?"

"I guess not. But we're taking a lot of risks now. If any one point of the plan goes wrong, we'll lose him."

"Then we'll just have to find him again. He'd contact me eventually."

She lifted her head, her eyes dark with apprehension. "I can't wait that long. I want this over. I'm tired of it hanging over our heads."

He hugged her and kissed her gently. "Me, too."

When he would have deepened the kiss, she propped herself up on her elbow. "Still, this ordeal has had its moments. You should have seen the expression on Max's face when he spotted the earl at that meeting. He looked like he'd been handed the keys to Fort Knox."

"I'm sure."

She gave a faint smile. "How 'bout ole Pops? He handled the scene like a pro."

Trevor couldn't suppress a wince. "You didn't call him that, did you?"

"You're not worried about twenty grand, but you're concerned how I address your father?"

He thought about it for ten seconds. "Yes."

"I called him what he asked me to—Henry."

And that was a marvel in itself. "I've never seen him be so charmed by anybody in my life. But then you're pretty cute."

"Cute?"

He traced her jawline with his finger. "Stunning. Brave." Wrapping his hand around the back of her neck, he pulled her close. "Irresistible."

She laid her mouth on his, exploring at first, then increasing the intensity. Her lips were sweeter than any dessert ever conceived, even in her clever mind. He'd never tire of the scent, feel and taste of her.

She pressed her feminine heat against his erection. He groaned and fumbled for the condoms in the bedside table's drawer, but she snagged his wrist, pining his hands above his head.

"Let me," she whispered before she proceeded to destroy his self-control with her mouth and body.

Passion flowed from every part of her. Her breath was hot and ragged as she kissed her way down his throat. She glided her tongue teasingly over his nipples, and he hardened to the point of near explosion.

When she rolled on the condom, she took her time doing so.

Meanwhile, he was using every ounce of willpower he had. But when she lifted her hips and welcomed him inside her body, the glorious pleasure of it overtook everything.

How was it possible to want somebody so much? To need to the point that nothing else existed but her?

They moved together as if born to be joined, and when he

climaxed, her moans of satisfaction sparked explosions like the aftershocks of a violent earthquake.

Love deluged him with its wondrous power when she collapsed on top of him, her heart galloping in time with his own.

So beautiful and perfect.

Nothing could part them.

_16_

"THE MONEY'S IN HIS personal account."

Trevor made the announcement to the gathered gang in Shelby's kitchen on Saturday morning.

Panic not relief jolted through Shelby. They were one step closer to meting out justice, and when the ax fell, Trevor's brother would be broken, defeated, forced to repay the swindled funds and jailed.

Wasn't that the vision she'd dreamed of for months? Even years?

So why was she sick inside? Why wasn't she thrilled?

"Hot damn," Victoria said from her perch on the counter.

"What's next?" Calla asked, her tone excited.

No one seemed to notice Shelby was on the verge of tears or that she'd clutched her hands together to keep them from shaking.

"We go to Detective Antonio and tell him everything," Trevor said. "The personal deposit is enough to bring Max in for questioning. Added to everything else, probably an arrest."

"Probably?" Shelby jumped on the word.

He frowned, whether because he sensed her tension or from her abrupt tone, she wasn't sure. "It's obviously not up to us, and at this point, we need help from the police. They need to get court orders to freeze Max's accounts."

"I agree with Trevor," Victoria said with a decisive nod. "What if Max decides to take off with the money?"

"Do you agree, sir?" Trevor asked his father.

Looking tired, Henry nodded. "I'm resigned to the idea that Max has to be stopped from ruining any more lives. I'll hire an attorney for him. Right after I give him the dressing-down of his life."

Calla gave Shelby a brief hug. "We set him up. It's time for Detective Antonio to take him down."

Yes, she wanted this over, but she was terrified that when it was, she would lose Trevor. They'd begun with lies. They'd bonded over revenge. Who'd want to build on that? "I think we should watch him another day or two."

Trevor approached her and took her hands in his. "Let's be done with all this. I know you're ready."

"What if we haven't done enough?" *What if I've gone too far?*

"Your family would be proud," Henry said. He winked at her. "Though I'm a bit sad to see my days as a gullible mark come to an end. I believe I could have had a nice career in the theater."

"Lord Aberforth is always looking for patrons for his son's plays," Trevor said drily. "Perhaps you could invest."

Henry's eyes widened. "Aberforth? That barking duffer? I wouldn't give him—" He stopped, obviously noticing Trevor's smile. "Very amusing, son."

Trevor and his father had become much closer over the last few days. Could she take some credit for that? Did it balance the bomb she'd dropped on the family?

Trevor turned back to Shelby. "The ending of the earl's acting career notwithstanding, wouldn't you be overjoyed to let this burden go? You've proved to the police that it's time to take this case seriously. Let them do their job."

She noted the antsy looks on her friends' faces. They'd given so much of themselves to her cause. She met Trevor's gaze and saw no hint of the foreboding brewing inside her. His eyes were clear, blue and perfect.

But for how much longer would he look at her that way?

She tried to smile. "You're right, of course. After all this time, it just feels strange to be near the end."

"Hot damn," Victoria said again, scooting off the counter and dropping to the floor. "I'm headed to the beach. Call me when they've got the jerk in custody." She sailed out the door.

"I'll call Detective Antonio," Calla said, hitching her purse on her shoulder.

"I'll do it," Trevor said. "He's going to be pretty annoyed. You shouldn't have to take the brunt of his anger again."

Calla glanced at the door Victoria had gone through. "You're sure?"

Trevor nodded. "Absolutely. Go to the beach."

"Bye." Calla ran after Victoria.

Fearing she might collapse under the weight of her dread, Shelby pulled away from Trevor. "I should get to work on the Perry wedding."

"Are you okay?"

"Fine." She nearly ran to the walk-in fridge. "I'm really behind with the prep."

He followed her. "Let me help."

"No." She frantically gathered produce at random. "Enjoy your Saturday. You and your father go to the park or something."

He slid his arms around her from behind and nuzzled her neck, exposed by the ponytail she'd gathered her hair into. "I'd rather stay here with you."

She nearly jumped out of her skin. "No! Thanks," she added in a softer voice.

None of these feelings for each other were real. He'd see that once Max was arrested, once there was nothing to secure them together. Once this mess hit the media, and his father relied on him to soothe the hole in his life and save the family name from total disgrace. He'd realize how different they were. He'd break her heart.

He drew her around to face him. "What's wrong?"

She couldn't meet his gaze. "Nothing." She skirted around him. "I just need to get to work."

"How about a celebration dinner tonight? Father, you should join us."

The earl nodded. "That sounds lovely. My last night in the city. Where do you recommend, Shelby?"

"Sorry, I can't go," Shelby said, laying out her ingredients and having absolutely no clue what she was going to do with them. "The wedding, remember?"

"We can help," Trevor said. "The Banfield men look quite dashing in a tuxedo."

"Don't be silly." Shelby drew a knife from the block and began chopping celery. "You guys go and have fun. Take him to Giovanni's."

Trevor exchanged a look with his father. "Maybe it's best if Shelby doesn't come. You should see Mario, the chef, trip over himself to please her."

Shelby rolled her eyes as Trevor no doubt expected her to. "Oh, good grief. That's such an exaggeration."

Trevor leaned toward her, brushing his lips over her cheek. "Not by much. He needs to be reminded you belong to me."

The desire and possessiveness in his eyes made her heart contract. Her throat threatened to close. She couldn't hold on much longer. "I'm sure you'll be happy to tell him."

"Count on it. You sure you don't want help?"

She pointed the knife at him. "Out."

Laughing, he held up his hands. "I'm going, Chef. I'm going. Call me later." After one last kiss, he and his father left the kitchen.

When she heard the door close behind them, the tears she'd been fighting fell unheeded. Under the weight of her sorrow, she collapsed into a chair and cried.

Project Robin Hood, Day Twenty-nine
Offices of Banfield Transportation

"He's withdrawing the money."

"What?" Trevor was sure he'd misheard his friend from the bank. "How? When?"

"Now."

"All of it?"

"He's closing the account. Wants five thousand in cash, and the rest in a cashier's check. What do I do?"

"Stall."

Trevor slammed down the phone, raced past Florence, then hailed a cab outside his building. "First Union Bank, on 5th," he said to the cabbie. "Quickly, please."

While he cursed himself for having not anticipated this turn of events, his heart pounded and reminded him Max's sudden flight wasn't the only problem he would have to face that day.

Shelby was running from him, too.

She'd claimed exhaustion on Saturday night after the wedding she'd catered. Yesterday she'd gone to brunch with him and his father, but she'd been distracted and jumpy, then told him he should spend time with his father, since his flight was departing that afternoon.

Last night, though she'd spent the night at his apartment,

she seemed to be going through the motions when they made love, and she'd been up and gone at dawn this morning.

She should be happy, eager to celebrate their victory. What was wrong? Had he done something to upset her? He'd gone through everything that had happened over the last few days, and, while stressful, he couldn't see what could have caused such a turnaround.

And now, if Max got away, would she blame him? Would they spend all their time looking for him? Instead of after-sex cuddling would they worry and plan their next move for revenge?

The possibility made him want to bang his head against something solid.

When he reached the bank, his friend was standing on the sidewalk out front.

"I'm sorry," he said when the cab pulled to the curb and Trevor opened the door. "We tried to go slow, but he's insistent and agitated. My clerk is putting the cash in stacks now. He'll be coming out any minute."

"It's okay. Go back inside. I'll follow him from here."

"Good luck."

Trevor nodded and ducked back in the cab. Reaching into his wallet, he pulled out a wad of twenties and handed them to the driver. "Could you wait at the end of the block?"

"You got it, pal."

He should call Shelby, but his mind was racing so quickly, he couldn't think what to say. Using the side mirror, he kept watch on the bank's front door, and nearly fell off the seat when Max exited, looking around furtively and toting a brown leather briefcase.

Trevor had the faint, irrational impulse to laugh. When had his life become a spy movie?

"Get ready to go," he said to the cabbie, watching Max raise his hand to hail a cab.

Trevor's driver did a professional job of getting in line a few cars behind Max's cab. As they inched through midday traffic, he called Shelby and explained what was happening.

"We should have been watching him," she said, her voice low and strained.

"Too late to regret it now. Call Victoria and tell her to come get you, then ring me back, and I'll update you on where I am."

"Okay. What are we going to do if we catch up to him?"

Frustrated and edgy, Trevor speared his hand through his hair. "I have no idea."

"We'll think of something." She paused, then added in a shaky voice, "I'm so sorry, Trevor. This is all my fault."

"It's *not*," he said firmly. "Call Victoria."

He disconnected and let his head fall back against the seat.

"You need the cops, buddy?" the cabbie asked.

"Among other things," Trevor said bleakly. "Don't lose that cab, and you can be part of the big bust."

"Cool."

In true NYC style, he was thrilled to be part of the action instead of intimidated by the possibility of danger.

"Where are you?" Shelby asked when she called a few minutes later.

"That was fast."

"Victoria and Calla were already on their way here."

"I'm going through the Midtown Tunnel."

"He's headed to Queens? What—" She stopped. "He's going to LaGuardia."

"It would make sense."

"It doesn't actually, but we're right behind you. Call when you know for sure."

"That the cops?" the cabbie asked, weaving around a bus to keep Max's cab in sight.

"My girlfriend."

"And she's a cop?"

"She's a caterer."

"Uh-huh."

"I promise I'll buy you a beer later and tell you the whole story."

"Ought to be a doozy." The cabbie met his gaze in the rearview mirror. "Mind if I ask who we're followin'?"

"My brother."

"Better make it two beers."

Max was indeed headed to the airport. The ladies caught up to Trevor's cab, so he was able to wave to them through the back window. Victoria looked determined, Shelby worried and Calla was on the phone—no doubt with Detective Antonio.

Trevor had called the detective himself but had only gotten his voice mail. Maybe Calla was having better luck.

What was Max thinking? What was he *doing?*

With the bank account on watch, they'd called off the surveillance on Max. None of them had had any contact with him all weekend. What could have spooked him to send him running to the airport with a briefcase full of cash?

At the airport curb, Trevor gave the cabbie his card. "Thanks. Call me and I'll tell you how it turns out."

"Appreciate it, but I think I can guess." He turned and pointed to a car a little ways ahead—one Detective Devin Antonio was alighting from accompanied by two other men. "Those your cops?"

"Yeah. Thanks again."

They'd been waiting on Max's arrival. How had they known he was coming?

"That's Antonio," Shelby said, jogging up beside him.

He linked their hands. "Come on."

They rushed through the sliding doors with Victoria and

Calla right behind them. Victoria's car was sure to get towed, but none of them cared.

Max was hustling toward the security line as if the devil himself were on his heels, which—though his brother might not yet realize it—he was.

How he thought he'd get through with a suitcase full of cash, Trevor had no idea. Panic and bad judgment were Max's forte.

Badges flipped out, Antonio and his compatriots approached Max. He stumbled and tried to look shocked and innocent, though he was clearly sweating and guilty. Smooth as silk, the cops took him by his arms and relieved him of the briefcase, escorting him to the far end of the facility with only a few passengers and airline employees even noticing the disturbance.

As Detective Antonio and his group approached a door tucked behind one of the airline check-ins, Trevor walked up to them. "Good afternoon, Detective. You've been busy."

"Well, well, if it isn't the Nosy Caterer and her band of happy chicks." He smiled sardonically at Trevor. "Plus one rooster."

Trevor knew their chances of getting information out of the police were brief, so he held his reaction to Antonio's insult in check. "Do you mind if we tag along? We've been trying to get in touch with you."

"Yeah, I got your messages." His gaze swept the group, pausing ever-so-briefly on Calla. "Come on."

One of the guys with Antonio opened the door with a key card, then led them all inside the airport security offices. With little fanfare, they moved past the main desk and down a hall.

That's when Max's head whipped around. He glared at Trevor as he struggled like a scalded cat. The cops on either side, being bigger, stronger and obviously experienced with various criminals, subdued and cuffed him with almost no effort.

"You!" Max screamed at Trevor. "You did this."

"Swindled millions through nonexistent investment schemes?" Trevor lifted his eyebrows. "I don't think so, dear brother."

"You're such an idiot." Max's mouth twisted, his eyes glittered with rage. "You don't know half of what I've done. I can get away with anything I want. I'm the future earl."

In shock, Trevor found no clever words came to his lips. The brother he knew, the charming, not-so-clever boy had fallen away, leaving a desperate, hate-filled crook.

"And *her*." Max jerked his head toward Shelby. "I knew exactly who she was at the condo meeting. That's why I decided to cash out and go back to London. These cops can't touch me there."

In his rage, Max had somehow failed to grasp that he was very much in American custody and getting to London wouldn't be as easy as strolling onto a jet.

"I helped you because you're family," Trevor said, keeping his tone even, though he felt as if he'd been punched in the stomach. "How could you do this to Father?"

His face mottled, Max lunged toward Trevor, only to have the cops subdue him once again. "Traitor! That's what you are. I don't know what you said to Father to get him to go along with your stupid little domestic there, but you can bet I'll tell him all about your ridiculous traps. He'll have me out of here in less than an hour."

Trevor pitied him, since he knew that wasn't going to happen. But he also longed to strike back. Nobody insulted Shelby.

And they still had the winning hand. While Max might have recognized Shelby, their plan had accomplished its goal—Max was right where he belonged.

Leaning toward his brother, Trevor let his own fury show. "You can bet I've learned my lesson about helping you. You're on your own from now on."

"*Wrong.* I can't wait to watch Father force you to clean up behind me. Again." Max laughed as the cops forced him down the hall. "See you soon, little brother."

In the midst of his disappointment and anger, Trevor had the odd sensation of being tossed back in time.

He recalled a birthday he was supposed to spend with his mother, but instead had been jarringly sent back to Westmore Manor because his mother had decided to spend the time in Puerto Rico with her latest lover.

The earl had welcomed Trevor back home with his usual dignity and restrained pleasure. Max, however, hadn't been the least thrilled.

Resentment had flashed in Max's eyes. He'd clearly wanted Father, and the attention, all to himself.

Should they have figured out then how far down he would go, how greedy and lacking in conscience he'd eventually become? Maybe Trevor would ask himself that question for the rest of his life.

Shelby squeezed his hand, bringing him back to reality.

He wrapped his arm around her shoulders and held on. Max had made his own bed. *She* was his future.

"Always liked a good family reunion," Antonio commented.

The detective took Trevor, Shelby and her friends into one room, while the other two cops ushered Max into another one.

"How did you find him?" the detective asked, standing while everyone else found a seat in the small conference room.

"How did you know he was coming here?" Trevor returned.

Antonio shook his head. "You first."

Even with chicks and a rooster present, Trevor wasn't in the mood for a game of chicken. He only wanted to know what was going to happen now.

So he recounted the condo-development project and the trap they'd subsequently laid for Max.

"Inside connections at the bank, huh?" Antonio nodded. "Not bad—for civis."

"And we'll be perfectly happy to go back to being civilians," Shelby said, "if you'll tell us why you're finally arresting Max."

The detective propped his hip on the table. "Oh, I have a long list of charges I'll be filing. While you people were attending fancy parties at the hotel and doing some really obvious and lousy surveillance, I was doing my job."

Calla gave him a shaky smile. "We never doubted you—"

"What do you mean lousy surveillance?" Victoria broke in.

"Nice car," he answered. "The salary difference between PR execs and cops is a crying shame."

"Detective, please." Shelby's hands were clenched so tightly, her knuckles had turned white. "What's going on?"

Trevor laid his hand on Shelby's thigh as Antonio explained what he'd been doing while the Robin Hood gang was organizing their sting operation.

Based on Mrs. Rosenburg's complaint, plus the evidence Shelby had gathered, he'd gotten a court order to search and bug Max's office, which allowed them to learn about Max's gambling problem.

In addition to swindles and schemes, which the police had gotten his bank records to prove, he'd borrowed against the value of the hotel to pay off heavy gambling debts. The detective was certain he could bring Max in for questioning and get a confession, since, with the questionable people he owed money to, jail was the safest place for him.

"But Max got a call from his bookie this morning, warning

him that he'd run out of patience. Max, who'd spent the last few days preparing for a trip, buying a one-way plane ticket to London, cashing checks at various banks all over town, hung up and called the airline to move up his flight to today." The detective shrugged. "I decided it was time to show my hand."

Trevor looked at the women around him, all stunned and just a bit disappointed. While they'd thought they were so clever with their disguises and vigilante plans, the police had been quietly building their case all along. Their surveillance had been organized, sophisticated and yielded actual results.

Antonio sensed their letdown. "The fact that he's got all this stolen cash on him will add to my case, though, so nice job there. And now I know why he was planning to head to London in the first place—more bad disguises on Miss Dixon."

"So we helped," Calla said slowly.

"Sure. I'll let Miss Dixon's parents know when Banfield's assets have been sold off. They should get their original investment back." The detective scowled. "But do me a favor and go back to your catering, writing, advertising, transporting and whatever. This kind of thing is best left to the professionals."

A GLASS OF SCOTCH IN his hands, Trevor watched Shelby pace his living room.

"Do you think we helped at all?" she asked. "Or was Antonio just blowing smoke up our skirts?"

"I'm not wearing a skirt." And the shock of seeing his brother's complete lack of conscience had him way more agitated than the detective's thorough and professional investigation. "Sit down and have a drink with me."

She looked at his extended hand, then away. "Don't you want to go see him?"

"I called a lawyer, just as my father asked me to. Max will

likely spend the night in jail and be arraigned in the morning. He may have to stay there until the trial, considering he's a flight risk."

"And you're not upset?"

"Hell, yes, I'm upset. Come here and comfort me."

He'd said it to make her smile. She didn't.

She crossed her arms over her middle, as if she were ill. "I can't be a countess."

He set aside his glass. "A countess? What are you talking about?"

"Max is going to jail. Won't he get disinherited or something? You'll be the earl. You have to go out with ladies, maybe even princesses. I'm not either."

Her voice had risen to a high-strung pitch. He leaned forward, resting his arms on his thighs. At least he knew what had been bothering her the last few days. "Max won't be disinherited. The title will come to him on my father's death, even if he's in prison. That's the law. My father's hale and hearty, as you've seen, by the way. What's this really about?"

"We're too different. We're never going to work out. You're nobility. I'm a caterer."

He fought to hold on to his patience. Whatever reaction he'd expected from her, this certainly wasn't it. He'd put a bottle of champagne in the icebox, for pity's sake. "I'm not nobility, as I've explained several times. I'm a man. One who—"

"A mogul, then. Wouldn't your father be happier if you dated a polished English lady?"

The grim finality in her tone pushed him to his feet. "My father genuinely likes you, as if that even matters." He tried to draw her into his arms, but she jerked back, and a fissure of panic darted through him.

His touch rejected, he slid his hands in the pockets of his slacks. "You're very much a lady, and I'll buy you a damn crown if you want to be a princess."

Her gaze flew to his. "No. I don't." She whirled away. "We don't belong together."

His heart stopped for several beats.

"You can see that, can't you?" she asked, rushing on, unaware that her doubt was crushing him. She flung her arms in the air as she faced him again. "We have nothing in common. I don't belong in this place. You volunteered yourself and *the Earl of Westmore* as tuxedoed waiters for one of my catering events. I can't do that to you. It isn't right."

"Neither I, nor the bloody Earl of Westmore, are afraid of hard work."

"That's not what I mean." Tears flooded her eyes. "I got your brother arrested. Have you already forgotten that?"

"You're not putting Max between us anymore. I helped put him there, and I don't regret it." On some level he understood her guilt. He should have done something about Max sooner. He should have understood how far his brother had fallen. But they shouldn't be blaming each other, they should be turning to each other, not away. "Can we not talk about him for once? For one night?"

"I don't see how."

"Sure you do. We change the subject." He walked to her, laying his hands on her shoulders. "I love you."

Fear, not happiness, leaped into her eyes. "You don't mean that. You're upset."

His heart breaking into pieces, he shot back, "I do mean it."

Had he honestly expected her to fall into his arms, confess her undying love and they'd live happily ever after?

Yes, he had.

"We started this relationship on a lie," she reminded him.

"I don't care."

"I do." She grabbed her bag off the coffee table and headed

down the hall. "We need some time apart. Time to figure out if this is real or not."

"I don't."

She turned, and a tear slid down her cheek. "I do."

He pressed his lips together to keep from begging her to stay. "I'll be here."

She said nothing, the door clicking shut her only response.

BREATHING AS IF SHE'D RUN a mile, Shelby stumbled out of the elevator and into the lobby of Trevor's building. "What am I doing?" she muttered. "Where am I going?"

He loved her. Seriously? *No freakin' kidding?*

Hope and happiness she hadn't let herself feel earlier washed over her. Trevor didn't say things he didn't mean. He didn't do things he didn't want to.

"Can I help you, Ms. Dixon?" Fred asked.

"I— No. I just— I need a minute."

She wandered to the front windows and pressed her forehead against the glass.

Her dreams had literally come true. Max in jail; Trevor returning her love.

Why was she panicking?

She was being flighty and unpredictable—exactly what she'd assured Henry she wasn't. And she definitely knew what she wanted. She wanted Trevor. Differences and all.

True, the journey to this point had been complicated. But if they could get through the ordeal with Max, starting on opposite sides with deceit and family loyalties between them, joining forces, compromising, surviving and still loving each other at the end... Well, it seemed they could likely get through anything.

True justice was illusive, but true love was easy. If she wanted to find it badly enough.

She was running, plain and simple. She wasn't weak like

Max. And if she had to wear a crown and learn to curtsy to be with Trevor, then that's what she'd do.

It's not wise to come between me and something I want, she'd once said to Henry.

It was time she proved her challenge.

Looking around, her gaze fell on the elevators.

She couldn't run back to him without overcoming one last obstacle. A sense of déjà vu washed over her.

Hadn't she once paced this same lobby, taking a chance on seeing Trevor again? On them finding a way to turn vengeance and mistrust into hope?

Humiliated, though that was the least of her worries, she walked toward the security desk. "Uh, Fred," she said, clearing her throat when her voice croaked out like a rusty wheel. "Can I go back up?"

Fred, naturally, looked utterly confused. "Well… I'm supposed to clear everybody, every time."

"But I'm a knight who's raised her sword to strike down the tyranny of injustice. I've rescued the princess from the castle and brought peace and hope to all the land." She leaned forward and whispered, "So I'd really like my reward now."

Fred was half smiling, half alarmed. "What reward?"

"The Honorable Trevor Banfield."

Whether he thought she was sincere or crazy, Fred nevertheless nodded. "Elevator three."

Impulsively—proving she might be unpredictable at times—she kissed his cheek. As she rushed to the elevator, she called over her shoulder, "Don't tell him I'm coming, please."

On the ride up, she remembered Trevor's face when she'd told him they didn't belong together. When he'd told her he loved her, and she hadn't believed him.

She'd hurt him.

Maybe he should have spent some of that tough love on his brother years ago.

But then they never would have met.

And that scenario absolutely didn't fit with her fairy tale.

When the elevator doors opened, Trevor, anxious, beautiful and determined, was standing there.

She blinked. "My lord."

He yanked her into his arms. "My love."

Then he was kissing her as if she was his whole world, as if he'd never let her go, no matter how far and fast she wanted to run.

He didn't know, at least not yet, that she wasn't going anywhere without him ever again.

Arms wrapped around each other, they shuffled into his apartment.

"Why'd you come back?" he asked, his mouth hot and hungry against her cheek.

"We spent enough time apart." She placed her hands on either side of his face. "And I think I might be a bit impulsive. Oh, and I love you, too. I think I forgot to mention that earlier."

The smile she adored blossomed on his face, and she wanted his lips on hers as soon as possible. And forever. "You definitely left that part out." He slid his arms around her waist. "Again, please."

She slid her arms around his neck. "I love you."

He kissed her, his devotion to her never more precious. "When I'm with you, I'm complete. I think I knew that from the first moment I touched you."

"And tasted my crab cakes."

His eyes gleamed. "That, too."

"No matter how fast this has happened, how unlikely a couple we might be, I believe in us." She slid her hand through his hair, relishing the silken texture, scarcely able to believe he was all hers. "This is real. The future could bring anything, but we'll face it together."

He hugged her tight against him. "That's what I call a good plan."

"My best."

"I wasn't kidding about my talent with tuxedos. I can always fill in as a waiter at one of your events."

"After I see you in this tuxedo, your lordship, I'll consider it."

"Consider, will you?"

"Well, the view without a tuxedo is pretty impressive, so I'm sure you'll do fine. In the meantime, we're overdue for a celebration. How are you at opening champagne?"

He grinned and guided her to the kitchen. "Why don't I demonstrate?"

* * * * *

PASSION

COMING NEXT MONTH
AVAILABLE MAY 29, 2012

REQUEST YOUR FREE BOOKS!
2 FREE NOVELS PLUS 2 FREE GIFTS!

♦Harlequin®

Blaze™

red-hot reads!

YES! Please send me 2 FREE Harlequin® Blaze™ novels and my 2 FREE gifts (gifts are worth about $10). After receiving them, if I don't wish to receive any more books, I can return the shipping statement marked "cancel." If I don't cancel, I will receive 6 brand-new novels every month and be billed just $4.49 per book in the U.S. or $4.96 per book in Canada. That's a saving of at least 14% off the cover price. It's quite a bargain. Shipping and handling is just 50¢ per book in the U.S. and 75¢ per book in Canada.* I understand that accepting the 2 free books and gifts places me under no obligation to buy anything. I can always return a shipment and cancel at any time. Even if I never buy another book, the two free books and gifts are mine to keep forever.

151/351 HDN FEQE

Name	(PLEASE PRINT)	

Address		Apt. #

City	State/Prov.	Zip/Postal Code

Signature (if under 18, a parent or guardian must sign)

Mail to the **Reader Service:**
IN U.S.A.: P.O. Box 1867, Buffalo, NY 14240-1867
IN CANADA: P.O. Box 609, Fort Erie, Ontario L2A 5X3

Not valid for current subscribers to Harlequin Blaze books.

Want to try two free books from another line?
Call 1-800-873-8635 or visit www.ReaderService.com.

* Terms and prices subject to change without notice. Prices do not include applicable taxes. Sales tax applicable in N.Y. Canadian residents will be charged applicable taxes. Offer not valid in Quebec. This offer is limited to one order per household. All orders subject to credit approval. Credit or debit balances in a customer's account(s) may be offset by any other outstanding balance owed by or to the customer. Please allow 4 to 6 weeks for delivery. Offer available while quantities last.

Your Privacy—The Reader Service is committed to protecting your privacy. Our Privacy Policy is available online at www.ReaderService.com or upon request from the Reader Service.

We make a portion of our mailing list available to reputable third parties that offer products we believe may interest you. If you prefer that we not exchange your name with third parties, or if you wish to clarify or modify your communication preferences, please visit us at www.ReaderService.com/consumerschoice or write to us at Reader Service Preference Service, P.O. Box 9062, Buffalo, NY 14269. Include your complete name and address.

Fall under the spell of fan-favorite author

Leslie Kelly

Workaholic Mimi Burdette thinks she's satisfied dating the handsome man her father has picked out for her. But when sexy firefighter Xander McKinley moves into her apartment building, Mimi finds herself becoming…distracted. When Mimi opens a fortune cookie predicting who will be the man of her dreams, then starts having erotic dreams, she never imagines Xander is having the same dreams! Until they come together and bring those dreams to life.

Blazing Midsummer Nights

The magic begins June 2012

Saddle up with Harlequin® series books this summer and find a cowboy for every mood!

Available wherever books are sold.

www.Harlequin.com

HB79693